W9-DGR-850

At First I Hope for Rescue

At First
I Hope
for
Rescue

HOLLEY RUBINSKY

ALFRED A. KNOPF CANADA

PUBLISHED BY ALFRED A. KNOPF CANADA

Copyright © 1997 by Holley Rubinsky

All rights reserved under International and
Pan American Copyright Conventions. Published in
Canada by Alfred A. Knopf Canada, Toronto, in 1997.
Distributed by Random House of Canada Limited, Toronto.

Canadian Cataloguing in Publication Data

Rubinsky, Holley, 1943 –
At first I hope for rescue

ISBN 0-676-97057-5

I. Title.

PS8585.U265A8   1997   C813'.54   C96-932141-4
PR9199.3.R82A8   1997

First Edition

Printed and bound in the United States of America

This book is for Yuri Rubinsky (1952 – 1996).
The one who would want most to
comfort me is the one I mourn.

ACKNOWLEDGEMENTS

My heartfelt gratitude to those who were steadfast in their support this year: foremost, Reiki Master Cheryl Kerman, many times brave; my mother, Ella Woolf, always in my corner; my daughter Robin Ballard, compassionately sensible, and her supportive husband Martin Rohner; my gourmet companion Stan Bevington, instrumental in founding the Yuri Rubinsky Insight Foundation; David Zieroth, for his counsel; my neighbour Marg McQuigan, who listened and archived; Sarah Berry, who, sadly, knew what to do; Marie and Bill Clarke, who were there when I needed them; and for their help at important junctures: Josi Abata, Elizabeth Abraham, Kathy Akehurst, Ian Brown, Sarah and Marc Giacomelli, Alistair and Anita MacLeod, Reiki Master Bernie Morin, Wendela and Al Zikovitz.

My thanks to the editors who published parts of this book, in earlier forms, in their magazines: *Descant*, *Event*, *Exile*, *Prairie Fire*, *Prism international*; and to Janine Cheeseman, Jennifer Glossop and Heather Henderson, who were first readers.

Special thanks to David Zieroth for invaluable editorial suggestions over the years and especially on this book, and for discovering the title of the collection; and a toast to Louise Dennys, both publisher and editor. Yuri said to wait and he was right.

CONTENTS

Necessary Balance/1

Algorithms/59

The Other Room/101

Fetish/143

Road's End/187

NECESSARY BALANCE

Bet Harker ✓

HEARSAY HAS IT THAT THE OLD HOUSE up across the road has been sold to newcomers, a family from Saskatoon or Sudbury or some such place. A few of us neighbours dodge into the yard to make off with flowers, seeds and bulbs, telling ourselves Eunice would want it that way, seeing as how she was born in the town of Ruth and most of us were too. Which is bull. Eunice never did share her flowers with anybody, friend or stranger. It's the way of the old maid, I guess, keeping the sweetness for yourself.

It is hot as pissing hell.

But I am thinking this way this Saturday morning, collecting apples from the ageing trees near the road and having oddball notions because I am not an old maid and sometimes wish I was. Would be easier, not having to deal with a useless mate and a shabby resort, no lake access, nothing but quiet, a few trees and cheap rates. You have to turn onto the road out front, follow it down a steep slope and cross the main highway to get to Judith Lake from our place. And as for the mountain view everybody's paying for these days, Cedar Hideaway has it, if you climb the ridge at the back of our place and stand in the right spot.

I'm in a mid-life crisis, an extension of the one that has been going on for years. Forty-six and still fooling with questions like what am I doing and what is the point of doing anything and what is the point in general. Started with five cottages, sixteen years later still have the same five, rustic as all hell, chock-a-block with character. To be fair, we did put in a camper site, which saved our skinny, and a raspberry patch where guests can pick their own. And we have a rural, neighbourly quality to our environment, what with the vintage houses on big lots across from us, that a lot of city people like.

My Clarence is older and not much for dancing. Last night at the Kinsmen Firewood-for-Seniors benefit at the Legion Hall we sat at a table with the usual crew, my best friend, Nan Carmichael, and her hubby, Larry, who owns Ruth's largest building supply, their oldest daughter, Karen, that Larry is teaching to ballroom dance — as though any kid today will ever need that particular skill, but to each his own — the gang from the ambulance station and a bachelor logger or two that hang around Clarence so they can all blow smoke and drink too much, birds of a feather. What do I expect, my thick-waisted, sausage-legged self stuffed into my new Sears catalogue summer dress, looking exactly my age? Some masculine attention maybe?

My friend Nan is the sinewy, nervous type, lavish golden-brown curls billowing around her small face. She's educated, besides — nearly two years at a college in New Westminster. She wears glasses, big ugly black-rimmed ones, that announce a seriousness of purpose despite the hair and the hip-hugger dress Larry has her decked out in.

Next to Clarence, Larry is my least favourite man. He has a thing about women; ever since puberty he's been proving how macho he is. Nan puts up with it and his possessiveness, because he's what our mothers called a good provider. Also, I suppose she loved him. They have four girls, three of them products of Larry's barefoot-and-pregnant theory of a woman's place. Karen, the oldest, is Nan's from an indiscretion early in the marriage. Nan's thinking it's time to tell Karen. Should have done it long ago, I say.

God, I sound grumpy. I wipe the sweat off my face with my sleeve and toss a few small apples to bony old Buttercup, our family retainer. Used to be, tourist kids rode her around a ring, it made a special treat for them and for their folks watching, taking photos. Horse is too old now. My three hardly bother with her any more. Kids today are fickle.

Fact is, I envy Nan sometimes for Larry. Despite my body type, I am light on my feet. The music starts, my feet start tapping. Buck Hammond's Swing Band were hot last night. Crowd pleasers, they do the big band tunes at the start and then, as the night goes on, they break down into the pandemonium that passes for music today. I watch Larry out there, Nan and him one of the first couples to hit the floor, naturally. Larry is a smooth dancer, debonair and commanding. To a foxtrot he sweeps Nan around the room, everybody watching, you can't help it, her so slim, him so elegant and energetic, so sure of himself; and for a second I forget what an ass he is and just want to be her. If I get lucky, he'll lean across Clarence and ask me to dance.

This is what I think as I fan my flushed face with a serviette and watch them, keeping my elbows off the unwiped table. The ambulance crew has moved over to a livelier bunch, some out-of-towners already partying hard. Nan's girl Karen is a few seats down from me, staring at her fingernails. She hasn't clapped eyes on anybody so far, distancing herself from us old folks like any normal kid. She's a loner, a bit sullen, but pretty, has her mother's shape. There aren't many kids around; because of liquor being sold they can't get in without their parents, no fun for them. Then I notice one of Clarence's reprobate pals across from us drawing a bead on her and I slap my hand on the table to get his attention. "What do you think you're looking at, fool?" I say, and he gives me a startled look like I was his conscience materialized and about knocks his chair over, beating a retreat.

Karen glances sideways at me. "They're all just interested in one thing," she says and goes back to examining her nails.

Her remark makes my ears prickle. I fan myself faster, taken aback that I just heard a sixteen-year-old that I've known since Nan was carrying her, a girl the age of my daughter, Bethany, sound like some used-up tart. "Guys whatever age, they like the pretty girls, always have," I philosophize.

"It's not that, Auntie Bet" — using her childhood name for me — "it's just that men can tell stuff. About me. Oh, shit," she says as Larry and Nan swoop down upon us, Larry giving Nan one last twirl into her chair. She laughs,

6

slightly breathless, casts an apologetic glance in my direction. She knows I'd give an eye tooth to be out there on the floor — I'm a better dancer than she is — and I know she feels sorry for me, a wallflower same as I was in high school. My heart takes a little leap as Larry hovers. When he bows, I look up expectantly, can't help myself, lost for a moment in a Cinderella fantasy. Then he presents his arm to Karen. She takes her time standing, smooths the back of her skirt over her cute little butt and throws me a wink, a gesture I find baffling.

The horse gives a chuff, reminding me she'd like a few more apples, but I am cooked by the sun. As I head up the drive, the MacFarlane car comes shooting along, blowing dust on me. I put the plastic bags down and wave in a friendly, forgiving manner. What the hell, eh? Families like them are our bread and butter, booking for two weeks every year, regular as clockwork.

Lightly dusted, I feel like myself living my real life. I am made uneasy by the longings that dances set loose.

The apples are for tomorrow, for the fresh fruit and brandy compote to take on our annual Labour Day cruise — just the four of us, Nan and Larry, Clarence and me. Larry pays for the boat. The cruise, his idea a few years back when he became prosperous at the store, gives him a yearly opportunity to rub in the fact that Clarence and me continue our little plod plod up at Cedar Hideaway, same as we always have, never better, never worse. In the late spring and through summer I bust my butt with guests coming and going — beds to change, toilets to scrub. Labour Day is the beginning of the end, with different concerns as winter comes on. I look forward to the cruise, that official downshifting in my seasonal cycle of worry. Two long and luxurious days on the water is fun, even with Clarence sucking his bottle and Larry bragging about this and that. Nan and I aft, fishing, and Nan this year will be smoking instead of chewing on toothpicks — she's taken up smoking again and Larry is actually letting her, hasn't said a peep so far as I know and I usually manage to know things — and I'll be glugging dry beer (the blue-eyed blonde in the old TV ads sold me) and Nan'll be into Scotch, and later, after dusk, we'll be on a beach, grilling four perfect T-bone steaks, medium rare, on that we all agree.

Hell, you bet I'm ready, I think to myself as I kick open the laundry-room door and step into sloppy bubbles from an overflowing washing machine. My twins Jay and Jerry do the laundry but just try to get it into their thick heads that one-third cup of the liquid detergent brought by our new supplier really, truly, is enough. Twice we've been through this. They'll remember when they're cleaning up the overflow once I lay my hands on them and they'll flip their hair out of their eyes and mutter things like "Jeez, Mom, whyn't you remind us?" and life will continue on in this unfair manner until they graduate from high school, assuming I can bully them through high school, after which I kick their lazy butts out the door.

I need a holiday. I can't even be bothered to find the buggers and so I swab the mess myself with the string mop

8

and throw the sheets into the basin and rinse them by hand
and twist them until my hands ache — the machine won't
go into rinse or spin, it's clogged or some damn thing, and
a guest has use of the other — and while I'm looking out
the tiny grimy window covered with cobwebs (and one
fresh web from an obviously retarded and doomed little
garden spider), I wonder, I just plain wonder. My life
wasn't supposed to be like this, and I guess it is like this
because I didn't formulate an actual plan. My planning
got as far as me lying around with my eyes closed pictur-
ing my captivating self in a red dress in a grand ballroom
some place posh while rich, handsome fellows fell all over
themselves. It's this spineless, passive ambition you want
to spare your kids from. It leads to a life you never in your
dullest moments imagined. What you get is so utterly ordinary you're never convinced it's the deep-down you. Another sigh as I haul the sheets out to the line. There's only
one working dryer, and guests have first dibs.

The phone bell outside the shed ring-rings. I expect
Clarence to get it but he doesn't, I don't know where he's
got to, and I set down the basket, make a dash to the house.
It's Nan with two shades of news. She's into a breathy,
fawning voice. I don't know what is going on with her
lately; if she wasn't my best friend I don't think I could
stand her. "Larry says we might as well pick up our boat
from Dave Laws while we're at Green Willow Bay and
bring her back down ourselves. Dave's fixed the motor. It's
one hundred per cent now, Larry says. Dave stopped by
the store. Great, eh?"

Yuh, I can get behind it, as the kids say. Nan and I have had some good times in the eight-foot aluminum car topper that a family left behind two summers ago, when they bought a bigger boat. Nan and I found a used outboard motor for it, a four-horse Merc. We use our little car topper whenever we both get a couple of hours free — it stays at the ready, on Nan's beach, covered with a tarp. The motor is light enough for me to carry it from her shed, which I do while she loads the oars and fishing rods. I roll up my jeans, wade into the water, hoist the motor onto the back. My feet are callused and tough, the stones underfoot don't bother me. Nan climbs in, helps screw the Merc into position, I push us off, take my place aft. We're not serious about fishing, we play Trivial Pursuit (poles on their holders) while trolling, pop beers, talk kids, the guys, the usual gossip. Sometimes we actually catch a little trout.

But the Merc turned out to be erratic as sin and midway through this summer left us stranded, scaring us out of our knickers because we were on the far side when the blow caught us. We rowed and rowed and took on water and Nan bailed. I went to bed the whole next day with liniment on the arms and chest. We accepted Larry's suggestion about Dave Laws, north and across the lake at Green Willow Bay, who's a super mechanic and enough of a friend so he wouldn't charge much to repair it. My boys took the boat up on one of its good days and hitched a ride back. Dave's had it for weeks, Nan and I missing the summer, basically. I tell her okay, I'll bring the beer. She laughs, an uncertain twitter. "You won't believe it, and I'm so stressed about it I could just die, but Karen's coming along. On the cruise."

I notice the receiver smells of 3-in-1 oil. I check my hand, giving myself time to calm down. "Jesus, why?" My eye catches a receipt from the liquor store on the mess that passes for Clarence's desk. I am feeling suddenly explosive.

There's a tremor in her voice as she tells me Karen is grounded because she disobeyed Larry. She left the Legion dance early and didn't come home until two a.m. and the whole family had a terrible night, with Larry upset and Karen crying and Larry wanting to know the name of the boy she was sleeping with, he'd got it in his mind she was a slut, and the other girls were carrying on, Nan upstairs holding them, the whole thing was just awful, and so Larry doesn't trust leaving Karen at home on the long weekend because she'll spend it with some guy.

"Right," I say. "Man. What an asshole." The word I won't let my kids use just pops out.

"He's her *father*."

Of course Nan defends Larry, it's her thing. "Well, yeah, sorry. You sound wretched. Maybe he'd let her stay here. Gran Willits is coming. She could handle half a dozen snarky brats."

"Oh, I'll ask," Nan says brightly. "But don't you think that's wonderful about our boat?"

Sure. I hang up. She's not going to ask Larry anything, I can tell from her tone.

After supervising the kids with supper-dishes clean-up, I'm still in the kitchen packing the cooler when Larry and Clarence come stomping into the mud room. It's unusual that Clarence misses supper, so I suppose Larry's been leading him astray, it being the eve of the cruise. They're in pretty good spirits, all right, Larry carrying an open beer. They've come to pick up the bedding and utensils I've already packed to stash them on board, along with the box of booze, so we can get an early start in the morning.

I suppose I might've kept my mouth shut and avoided choking on my foot, but when Larry enters the kitchen, I mention that I know Karen's coming along, and then add, "We drink more than we ought when we're out there, eh? Maybe she shouldn't see us that way." Some glint in his eye has made me finish up with a lame argument, as though our drinking matters for anything. I feel unlike myself — cowed — and he hasn't even spoken. Clarence is behind him, the screen still open, mosquitoes darting in, his lips with that familiar looseness that drunks get that might explain why they can't form words very well. He's clueless to anything that's going on. And suddenly there is plenty going on between Larry and me.

Larry's moved, leaned himself against the counter on his arm, long legs crossed at the ankles. He looks at me, or rather, he looks in my direction, a handsome man that I had a crush on through school. I used to fantasize about him; I have a foolish side. Then I'd grown to feel sorry for him, because Clarence and I had two boys and a girl and he and Nan kept having girls. He used to drop over when my twins were playing peewee hockey, be goalie for them. This was when the Carmichaels lived along our road, before Larry built their big place on the water. I used to sit on the porch step and watch, admire his easiness with the kids. Little wild-haired, skinny-legged boys, tough and grubby as they come. *Mine*, I'd think.

But now there's no mistaking the air of patronizing patience in Larry. He doesn't bother replying. The attitude is he'll put up with a certain amount of female yapping, and I have had my little say. He changes his position, sidles towards Clarence, makes some crack I miss. I am not in the habit of kowtowing to anybody, and I reach for the dish towel behind me, a reassuring, domestic gesture, and try again: "It doesn't seem like a good idea, her being there. It'll spoil the trip."

Larry shakes his head, tsking, "Bet, Bet, Bet, Bet, Bet. Pet. Sweet Bet. You looked fab last night, cute dress. How come you wouldn't dance with me?"

"Yeah, how come?" mimics Clarence, emboldened by Larry's remark. Larry snickers and feints a punch or two at Clarence, then veers my way, his sweaty chest inches from my face. His shirt is creased near the top button where an iron has missed. He smells of coconut and beer. Suddenly he takes me in his arms and holds me in a mock swooning embrace. "This is what you miss, eh, sweet Bet. That lout's no use to a real woman." He's keeping an eye on Clarence as he plants a playful kiss on my cheek, then quickly slides his lips to mine and kisses me for real, slipping in the tip of his tongue. I turn the colours of the rainbow, I know, and

my efforts at getting free are half-hearted. The whole routine is reminiscent of the innocent fun we used to have in
younger days, but this doesn't feel right; the kiss is insult-
ing. Clarence says, "Hey, bub, my turn." I shake free of
Larry, glad for an excuse to focus on Clarence wearing his
goofy smile.

"That'll be the day," I say inanely and shoot him a
withering look, ignoring Larry grinning over my shoulder. "Take the goddamn box of booze to the truck, eh? I've
got better things to do than mess with you clowns."

"This gal was born bossy," Larry says. "We better hup
to, make a break for it." He flashes his most engaging grin.

I want us back in the normal spirit of things. In what I
intend as a teasing manner, I snap the end of the dishcloth
at Larry. The cloth hits his thigh; anger rises in his eyes,
which is how I feel too, the instant I recognize it in him. In
my warm kitchen there's a backdrop of menace, it's like the
first chill of winter. Larry laughs, followed by me and then
Clarence, the intent of our laughter to restore some kind of
necessary balance, the laughter itself shaky, thin and phony.

The next morning aboard the *Julia G*, Larry is jovial and
helpful, eager to get under way. Nan is cheerful (but then
Nan is always cheerful), Karen withdrawn but not sulky,
and Clarence, after a few too many last night, is looking
peaked but in his own way pleased as we cast off, the big
inboard rumbling. No Waves reads the buoy in the bay but
of course Larry ignores that, heads out fast, giving the
boats in their slips a few slaps.

Larry's trying to make up for us only having two days and one overnight this year because he was too busy at the store to take Saturday off. He's compensated royally; the *Julia G* is bigger and fancier than any cruiser we've had before. She's brass and blue carpet and real tiles in the head and a full-size shower. The galley's loaded: microwave, toaster, oven, stove, ceramic dishes, wineglasses even, the kind with stems. Clarence and I have a carpeted cabin with two berths, as do Larry and Nan; Karen will sleep on the pull-down in the dining area. Nan and I put the ice-chest foods into the fridge, make beds and move a few things around. I notice she doesn't ask Karen to help; they hardly look at each other. As far as I am concerned, the girl can sit inside and read *People* magazines until her eyes drop out, as long as she doesn't bring a cloud of gloom over the proceedings. She's wearing a pair of wrinkled red shorts and an oversized transparent blouse barely disguising a halter that shows off her cleavage. She sits at the end of the table, legs crossed, one swinging so that Nan and I are always aware of her presence as we chitchat and organize silverware and pots and pans.

The whole of Sunday glides along, sun and naps and peace. Judith is a tranquil lake in a good mood. We zigzag through the glistening surface of her calm, dark-denim blueness, moseying into creek mouths and coves because the guys want to explore old mine sites through binoculars. At twilight we lay anchor at Galena Creek. I step down the aft ladder, plop in — the water is chest-deep and colder than I expected — and then Larry does a bellyflop, acting the clown, and we're laughing and howling, splashing like kids before puberty strikes. Clarence won't join us; he's nursing a rye, and Nan doesn't want to get her hair wet. After a bit, we climb back aboard and Larry eases the *Julia G* closer to shore. The gang of us manage to lay the plank from the bow to a fairly flat rock and Karen comes gambolling down like a sure-footed mountain goat, making Nan and me roll our eyes; for us, the plank walk has been a balancing act. After supper and more drinks, we sit around the fire, flames dancing on our faces, and we look younger than we are, and peaceful.

Monday morning after breakfast — in the galley Nan pulls off fruit crêpes with whipped cream and Clarence insists on his usual, coffee boiled on the beach in a pot as dark as sin — Nan and I scoot up the short trail to Galena Falls, passing the ruin of a cabin overgrown with moss. The waterfall is tame compared to what it would be during the spring run-off, but still, the spray is like diamonds, the way the clear light of end-of-summer heightens everything. On the way back, we collect moss for my Hallowe'en Moss Woman costume. It's a concept that appeals to me.

Dave and Helen Laws named their inn Green Willow Bay, and even without having a proper bay, on the navigation map of Judith Lake their sheltered docks are called by that name. Everything they do is right; when we tie up early in the afternoon, cold beer in coolers waits for us under an umbrella on the lawn, seasoned hamburger patties are ready for the grill, an assortment of homemade condiments is spread on the table. They're politely solicitous about Karen, who stays on board. They're an odd pair, really, Dave and Helen, him with grime permanently under his nails and a rough-hewn sort of face and her so fine-boned and dainty but with what's called British grit. They've done a tip-top job restoring and redeveloping the property, and their success niggles at me. On Thursdays in summer, they serve tea and cakes at three p.m. and everybody, even locals, comes flocking up the oiled gravel road for the pleasure of sitting on the wide veranda of the main house, the view sweeping across manicured lawn and rose beds, onward to the lake and the hazy silhouettes of mountains beyond.

After burgers and beer, we split up, and I wander towards the dock, to get the fruit compote I left in the fridge of the *Julia G.* I detour by the boathouse to inspect the little car topper. Dave's so thorough in his repairs, he's even polished the outboard's cover. I run my hands over its smooth black hood and think, foolishly as it turns out, that it will be a grand finish to the cruise, Nan and me taking our little boat back to Ruth with the guys coming along behind.

It's my bare feet that surprises them, that and my lighter-than-she-looks way of moving. I say "them", because what I see when I bounce down the steps to the galley is two people embracing — what I should say, of course, is that I surprise him, I am interrupting *him*; she is just a child.

I spin around, whack my toe on a step, flee. Embarrassed, awkward and dumb, an intruder — until I'm back in the dimness of the boathouse and wondering why I am the one running. The boathouse smells of engine oil and old wood and the slimy green of trapped water. I pace the decking around the two slips, causing our little boat to rock, squint out at the lake, try to think. It isn't often I don't know what to do. A part of me wants to run scream- ing up the manicured lawn and point a finger; another part lies stunned as somebody waiting for something awful to stop in order to get on with pretending it never hap- pened. I need a friend to talk to. I need Nan. I snort; I must be looped to have such a thought. I touch my throat, feel my rapid pulse beneath my fingers. There's dessert to get through before we can decently leave. No way in pissing hell am I going back aboard the *Julia G*, acting like every- thing is hunky-dory.

Larry, pretty smashed, is busy creating a good time, laughing loud, cracking jokes when I rejoin the group. He shoots me a look that confirms I am not out of my mind, after all; and my heart sinks. It's obvious he's not as far gone as he's making out. Nobody asks about the fruit com- pote; instead, Helen brings a fresh-baked wild blueberry pie, blueberries picked from behind their place, and I eat too much, it's what I always do, and Larry teases me about my second piece, just like he would if everything was nor- mal. And I don't respond any different. It's like a cat or something wilder has got my tongue. Nan, watching Larry and me, begins picking at her blouse the way she does sometimes. "Look at the lake. Whitecaps forming," she says; and then "Oh, too bad. It's too late to leave now."

Bull, I think. For a moment or two Larry takes her side, and I know why; no doubt he'd rather I was under his thumb on board the *Julia G*, where he can make nice, try to win me over, slough it off as fun. But he's being careful, I feel it, and get the message loud and clear: I am a time bomb. I slide him a look. The next thing I know, Larry's changed his mind and is herding us all to the dock, encouraging his two gals to get out on that lake and have a last fling at summer.

Dave brings the boat around and we off-load from the *Julia G* life jackets and a six-pack of beer. Clarence tosses me a flashlight. The trip should take forty-five minutes at the poky speed our motor goes. It will be dusk when we land at Nan's beach. The idea is that the *Julia G* will give us a head start and then come alongside and pilot us home. First the men want to check out blueprints for a pair of new woodland cottages Dave has designed. That means another round. They wave us off.

Nan is a great reader and in the past, when we were out in our little boat, she told me plots of novels, like from Margaret Laurence, the one about the housewife who left her family; Nan could tell a story so convincing you'd think she was making it up herself. I was always happy listening to her soft voice, us rocking gently, my eye occasionally to the west where the big storms flurry up from, the motor off. It was true you couldn't catch much just drifting, but you couldn't hear a story while trolling, either, and there we would be, rapt, each in her action and reaction and the breeze sweet, lines dangling, osprey hunting off our little bow, to the north and south of us beauty so breathtaking I couldn't describe it without sounding like every cliché in the book. Those were the best times.

Now, though we're in our usual places, she facing me from the bow and I aft, steering, the mood is tense. "I don't trust this thing," Nan says, throwing her cigarette butt overboard, eyeing the motor. She's uncomfortable, I can tell, avoids my gaze, thinks maybe it's the faint sun working through the increasing haze; thinks it's the idea of the coming dark that's making her skittish, making her fuss with the flashlight, testing it. But I think it's me, the energy of me beginning to focus as I steer us southward, keeping close to shore, to the narrow inlets where we can pull in if need be. Off in the distance, to our right, is the island. We'll go around the south end of it before crossing the lake to Ruth. What I am beginning to feel is like during fishing. Line twigs, you start reeling in, eyes fixed on the point where line meets water, from where the prize — the mystery — will emerge. Nan is that mystery. From the moment I caught Larry with Karen, I had one thought: *She has to have known. She knows.*

"Would you like your jacket? A beer, can I get you a beer?"

I shake my head.

"Aw, come on. I'll have one, too." She's simpering, as she's done around Larry the whole trip, when I think about it. Her way of keeping things on an even keel. *She knows. She has to know.*

I want us further from Green Willow Bay, further

down the east shore where there are no clusters of summer houses or the huge isolated cabins of rich people, and then I'm going to ask her, I'm going to confront her. Meanwhile, I bide my time, keep occupied with steering around occasional deadheads, with the coolish breeze on my face, the fresh smell of deep water. I look at the rock formations, how the cliffs fall away in some places, how a mini-avalanche is obvious in others, an occasional tree sprouting from between rocks, impossible to imagine where it finds soil for its roots.

She pops open a beer, offers it to me first. She drinks and burps, burping not her style; she's trying hard. She gushes, "Oh, wow, this is great. Isn't it just great, Bet? Isn't it fun?" I want to punch her, she is being so phony. I check beyond us to see how far we've come. Far enough. A seagull flaps past. I reach back, cut the motor, slide around to face her.

"What happened?" she cries. "Oh, Lord, I thought Dave fixed it. Oh, Lord, I knew it, I just knew it. You can't trust any of them." She half-rises in her panic — and she is genuinely panicked, I feel it down the length of the boat. Her fear, so raw, unsettles me. My look must give me away. Her eyes widen behind her glasses as it dawns on her I cut the motor deliberately. "Are you out of your mind? Oh, my God, get it started — please Bet, start the motor, get it started — "

When I don't respond, sit riveted to the seat watching her lose it, a splat of beer hits me in the face. "Get this damn thing started or I will scream," she says. "Do you hear me? I want to go home. I want to go home now. Now!"

I wipe beer out of my eyes and smooth it on my chin and forehead as though it's a fancy cream. I'm not angry about the beer — although maybe I am, I don't know. I just think, Home? She wants to go home to that smarmy mess she lives with? Puts up with? *Allows?*

"Jesus Christ. Pissing hell," I explode, and then I can't stand it, I climb over the life jackets and the middle plank, and without a word coming to mind that I can say aloud, I punch her on the shoulder. My hand in a loose fist just whips out and baps her. Her glasses fly off — I didn't hit her that hard, I couldn't have hit her *that* hard — but her glasses fly off and land with a kerplunk in the lake. I hear them over the roar in my head.

She slaps at me blindly. She's helpless without her glasses, I ought to know; I was with her when she got her first pair at fourteen. I stumble back to my place, the boat bobbing, the silence of no motor and the hungry lapping of the lake against our flanks finally getting through to me. It seems hours have gone by, the change in weather is so sudden. Clouds are sifting in from the west, moving down the mountains like fog. As I watch, one layer of trees on the far shore disappears.

I turn to Nan, willing myself to say something. She's trembling head to toe, hugging her jacket, blinking furiously. I remember her with her little girls, them dressed in lace and ribbons, she loved that stuff, she loved the doll aspect of baby girls; even their bibs had nylon lace trims. I remember the joint family barbecues over charcoal briquettes, before the days of gas, Nan watching Larry watching my boys, Nan watching Larry watch Karen after she'd told him the truth about Karen, Nan excitedly telling me she was pregnant again, maybe a boy this time, followed by her hysterectomy a few months later for fibroid tumours.

God. I am in over my head. Get that motor going. One leg against the seat for balance, I yank the cord. Nothing. I let out the choke a notch, give the cord a tug, let out another notch of choke and yank again. The motor sputters. I pump the fuel line, adjust knobs, swipe at angry tears, curse under my breath.

Flooded. Nan has a cigarette ready to light. "Don't," I say.

She drops the cigarette, steps on it obediently, a kid caught. Her hands cover her face. I turn on the flashlight, aim it skyward. In its halo I notice her pretty hair is frazzled, the ponytail escaping from its daisy-flower elastic. At first I hope for rescue, listen for the throb of the *Julia G.* Feel pissed off they haven't come for us. I hear Nan snivelling, "We're *friends*." Yuh. Such great friends she's keeping all the hurt to herself. I have a vision of me charging up to the old maid's place in my C-width boots and stomping on the flowers. What I can't kill by stomping, I'll pull out one frigging root at a time.

The North Star glimmers through a hole in the clouds. The flashlight flickers, fades, rouses itself, goes out. Typical Clarence. The scent of cedar — the smell that accompanies camp fires and crickets — bursts upon us. I am suddenly afraid, fear more than the darkness. Because Clarence will be buzzed out of his gourd and Larry will be at the wheel. Throttle up. A man with a lot to lose.

Nan Carmichael

THERE'S USUALLY A PARADE going down the line, after
he starts touching the first, but I covered her from him, I
kept her close to me. I never left her alone with him. I said,
"No, Daddy needs to rest, you come with me," and I said
to him, "No, we have things to do, we need to talk." And
that would scare him, because he would think I was telling
her or that I might. It was always in his eyes: that I might.

One day I just stopped working in the store. Larry
liked me to pitch in a few hours a week, it made for more
of a family business that our customers appreciated, but
I stopped. Right after I suspected about Karen and him.
At first I just kept an eye on him and watched the others.
I was a hawk mother, I had eyes in the back of my head,
so careful of where everybody was. He wasn't a bad man,
I knew what everybody would think, I read the magazines too. It's all over the place, it's partly why I never said
anything, either; you can't stand in a drugstore and look
at the racks without seeing an article or two on it, and
so what was the point? To embarrass Karen, in the first
place not his real daughter, his "biological daughter" as
they say today, and my husband, our whole family, make
us public spectacles when probably Joe Whoever up the
road is doing the same to his own? I could see it was a

problem and at first I thought of killing myself, that was my first thought.

Already here in Ruth we had a case of incest and I was not interested in my family being linked with that crowd. It was a retarded girl and her father, there was another girl in the family there too, and the older one, the slow one, got pregnant from her father. She was so naive, so dozy in her mind, that she told some girls at school she was having her father's baby; I don't know how she put it, actually, I try to imagine it, how she'd put it. Yuh, she'd say in answer to some question of why she was gaining weight — no they wouldn't ask her, they wouldn't care enough about her to care whether she was fat or not; she wasn't a popular girl, so why would they ask? Well, if she was sick, if she was physically barfing in the john, then they might ask her why, if she seemed to be doing that a lot, and she'd say right out and pleased as punch, I am going to have a baby. It's growing in me. And they — the girls in their sloppy T-shirts trying to look cool, studying themselves in the mirrors between classes, giving each other looks, raised eyebrows and the like, egging her on — they ask, And who's the father? Holding their breath, just dying to hear the name of the football hero and fearing to hear the name of one of their boyfriends (one of them, one of the girls, cursing herself already, Oh, I should have done it when he wanted, oh shit, I should have). All of them gruesomely titillated by the very idea of someone fifteen, *their very age*, being actually pregnant. Bells might ring and bombs drop but you couldn't have torn those girls away from that spot.

It's Daddy's! Our pleased-as-punch girl would beam, you know, smile ear to ear and blink her simple brown eyes, and everybody would be sick, just be sick all over their shoes, thinking of it, about it and how it could happen and where was the mother? This is what they said, people in town. Where was the mother and did she know? Of course she would know and she would be damn glad. Yes. Because she hates having sex with him because maybe he smells bad and won't take a shower. Anyway, I don't know about it, the case, but I watched the girl's belly grow and the girl herself becoming even more contented-looking and the mother left town, but left behind the other daughter, which I found hard to believe, that she would do that. Leave her babies. The girl especially, only nine. I don't know about the boys in the family. There were three of them, two older, the third one just past toddler age. You wonder if the older ones got in on it with their sister, I mean, it's inevitable somebody would wonder, wonder how deep the corruption in the family went. The older girl liked her daddy, obviously, I mean, she made no bones about it.

Imagine. I try to imagine how it happened, try to picture it. This girl, maybe it started when she was ten? Who knows, could be younger, just playing around at first and some kissing, blowing on their necks, which makes them giggle and curl up, and then he could lift her in his arms and snuggle her and then sit down again and he would have her then in his lap, against himself, and say things. Maybe: Daddy likes having his big girl on his lap. Maybe not. I don't know. I don't know how they do these things.

How they soften the girl up. I suppose just because he's Daddy, the bringer of all good things. Daddy is a password for little girls. Daddy, Daddy! they cry when he comes home. Daddy, Daddy! And run and hug him.

Even from age eleven, Karen teased him. "Daddy, Daddy," she'd say, and lunge at him, then veer off at the last second so he'd be standing there with his arms out, crouched, you know, waiting for her to jump into his arms and she wouldn't. She'd be giggling in the living room and he would have to go find her and the chase, for that's what it was, the chase would be on and she would tantalize him — I see it now but I didn't then. She would tantalize him like this until she was twelve or so and they would be wrestling on the living-room rug and I would come in, carrying a dishcloth or dust rag, I did all that domestic work earnestly, thoroughly, I believed a clean house was a good home, I believed all the truisms my mother taught me. There they'd be wrestling, sometimes her in her school uniform, the pleated plaid skirt pulled up to her hips, her panties showing, and him in the coveralls, just home from the store, rolling around and grabbing her, tickling her. And her with her blonde hair she was so proud of, loose and falling all over the rug, bobby pins falling out, her face flushed and beautiful, yes beautiful, even I could see that.

But I didn't think anything of it. Maybe it started then, when I went out to play bridge on Wednesdays and the next girl down, Amy, and her little sisters, Jane and Laura, were watching their shows on TV in the basement rec room and the two of them were left on their own. Full with the meals I cooked and maybe doing the dishes, he would help Karen when it was her turn sometimes, which should have triggered me to something, he hates doing the dishes but he would help her sometimes and she would bat her eyelashes at him: "Oh, thank you, kind sir," she would say with an accent, like the Southern accent my sister Rita Lee sometimes affects, "Oh, thank you, kind sir." I was out the door, pleased with how nice the family got along. I didn't see what she did as flirting, a way of getting back at me. But it was.

So then I suppose one thing led to another. It's hard to picture it, exactly, what happened next. How he got to the penis without scaring her. I mean, I remember as a girl seeing my father's penis, by accident, really, as he was pulling it, how they do after peeing sometimes, kind of shake it a bit? And I was shocked to see it in his hand, just a part of it, not the whole thing, I realize now, but of course I didn't know, and I thought it was big then. I don't know how old I was, maybe eye level. Eye level to it or maybe a little taller, but it looked dark in his pale hand, it looked dark and there seemed to be some hidden hair, I saw a snake of it, or thought I did. So I thought about it, what girl wouldn't? It was only natural, a little girl curious and taken by surprise, and I imagined it, and each time it got bigger and the screw of hair seemed more snakelike sticking out of his old white underpants. I say old because I realize now they were dingy, they hadn't been bleached properly or else they would have been whiter. Or maybe he wouldn't let my mother use bleach, you never know people's private affairs, what goes on between two people, even if you live with them. They might have been his favourite pair, like Larry has a shirt you had better not even touch, left over from his year at BCIT when he thought he was going to be a forest ranger but they flunked him in maths because he'd goofed off in high school and then he found out he didn't have the aptitude really to make it worthwhile to try again and then — of course, I am to blame, I have faced that, I got pregnant with her, with Karen, by a young guy, a stranger, while Larry was running a tree-planting crew in the Queen Charlottes, saving money for us, for taking over his grandfather's building supply business. A one-time roll in the hay that took — it's too easy to make a human being — and I was screwed by an out-of-town fire fighter, the year the mountains up and down the lake were burning and the air was so thick with bloody-coloured haze we might as well have been in hell. Stress, they'd say today, but it wasn't stress, I was horny, cooking two shifts a day up at the arena for a hundred sweaty men and I was twenty-five, old enough to know better but impatient and tired of Larry's promises. We were living in a cabin outside town, no running water, and I thought he had us living there just to bug me. My father had been mayor once.

I remember the unshaven roughness hurting my chin and cheeks, how my face stayed red afterwards as if I had a rash. I remember the smell of smoke and urgency on him. And how I sprang up from off the bag of flour I was propped against in the storage room, normally the women's hockey changing room, got up from behind the boxes of tinned chicken gravy and brushed off the back of my sleeveless summer dress, the stranger's hanky wadded in my panties. I turned him on because I reminded him of his sister (which makes you wonder about *his* family if you're thinking along those lines) — and I kissed him cavalierly, I think you could say, on the cheek and inhaled him and left. Shut the door, looked both ways down the hall and went back to the kitchen where just two of us were finishing up for the night, me and Marge Hill from the Zoo Café. I don't know what she thought or if she could smell the sex on me, if she found the length of my absence suspicious, and I said something to her about wiping the damn storeroom floor, someone had spilled coffee in there.

Now I would like to know his family's medical history, to see a picture of the sister I reminded him of, because I wonder, does Karen look like her? Does Karen have a whole genetic family she would have been happier in, maybe more at home in? Because among our other girls, she is the odd one out: fairer where they are dark, sharp-faced where they have their father's round features. I wonder if adopted people, whether they know they are or not, feel uneasy inside themselves.

My blood-sister Rita Lee always figured she was better than the rest of the boring family, so maybe having that thought isn't genetic. But the general heart shape of Karen's face, I don't know where it comes from; there's a mole on her left forearm that isn't in Larry's family or mine, at least in the ones still alive, there's the odd quirk, I guess you'd call it, of an eyebrow when she's sad; and maybe she'd have had one or more of those attributes if she were a hundred per cent ours, but I'll never know, Larry'll never know, nor will she, even if she finds out. At least I should have asked his name.

His town I know, he did tell me that, and it's two valleys over. I've thought of driving there and hanging out, looking for him or for a child that's his who looks a lot like my child, who would be her half-sibling. Hang out in a mall or the donut shop and wait for him, for an aunt, his mother, someone with a resemblance (assuming something about his appearance would be imprinted on me subliminally, I can't recall anything except the smell and feel, but you'd think a memory would be in my mind somewhere, the connection we'd made so elemental), wait for someone, anyway, with that mole — I would have to go in summer — sit eyes peeled, on the lookout for the distinctive mole. After all, if she were sick, if she got sick, we'd need a genuine medical history to solve something life-threatening and elusive. All through her growing up I prayed that she would stay healthy, a selfish kind of praying, because over at the clinic she carries a false history, in that Larry's mother with diabetes on her side of the family, for example, isn't Karen's grandmother, his dead father who was a drunk passed no genes on to her.

When I first began to suspect him — them — it was hard climbing into the same bed with him, acting like nothing was wrong. I let him kiss me, make love to me, all the while wondering about her, about the inside of her, if,

God forbid, they'd gone that far, how her vagina felt, what the difference was from mine inside. Lying beside him full of terrible questions and keeping mum. I started getting up and douching in the bathtub with a brand-new douche bag, not having bothered in years, most long-married women don't, but I wanted the remains of him out of me, I couldn't stand the idea of sharing his semen with my daughter, it made me sick to my stomach, the very idea. And that's when I started realizing about her being the one perpetrating whatever they were up to. She was a flirt, and I'd be thinking while lying in the bathtub, legs up, filling my cavity with Massengil or Betadine, the latter red and satisfying because my lower body'd be lying in it, the effluvium, in an awkward, uncomfortable position, torso balanced on elbows, trying to keep my back and shoulders dry; and then sitting up, watching the fluids burp out of me. Cleansing me of sins was the sense of it even though I wasn't a Catholic, sitting in this broth the colour of watered-down blood, goose bumps on my thin thighs, their shape still nice but the flesh loose with my age, my tailbone against the tub aching because that part of me is made funny, my tailbone juts out too far. Sitting in that mess in the night until I got cold and clammy and stepped out of the tub and dried off and tiptoed back to my husband's bed hating him, my teeth gritted against him, my throat aching from self-imposed silence.

Our kitchen was in a state of disrepair, things had been falling apart for years and I'd complained for years, for all the good it did. It was ironic, on the face of it, because Larry owned the building supply and had wholesale access to sinks and cupboards, counter tops, Maytag dishwashers (we didn't even have a dishwasher; we had daughters, didn't we? that was Larry's half-serious retort) and Armstrong no-wax vinyl I could have used, raising four girls, cooking for six every night. It was an embarrassment to me if we had people in and they got a glimpse of the kitchen. And he did like to have people in, he liked to entertain and show off the Hitachi thirty-two-inch TV and his satellite dish that was so small you'd have to look for it behind the ivy hugging the house. And our dining room was nice, good furniture I inherited from my parents, including a grandfather clock they had brought from Bavaria.

Bright and early Tuesday, the morning after the disastrous Labour Day cruise, Larry announced that we were renovating the kitchen. He had Amy, the oldest of our younger three, put the coffee on to perc and bring it to me in bed. I couldn't refuse, Larry wouldn't have it. He hopped in the truck and ran over to the store and brought back sample books, lugging armfuls of them into the house, getting the girls all excited: Lookee here, look at this. Amy, Jane and Laura were twittering around the bed — and I was wearing an old pair of glasses I didn't see out of all that well, lying there like a prisoner.

I knew when I was being sidetracked. What annoyed me was how he was using the girls, innocently excited about their dad's sudden plan. Mrs. Lepine, our French-Canadian neighbour, had stayed with them the two days. Right when we got in last night, Larry woke her to drive her home; he insisted he wanted just his family under his roof, ignoring that Karen took off to spend the night at a friend's house. She knew by my attitude towards her when we'd met up on the beach — late, Bet and I freezing and miserable after the *Julia G* just about ran us over, rescuing us — that I didn't care when I next saw her.

So now I was letting the girls flutter around me, bringing me tissues (I'd caught a terrible cold). For them, I got over my irritation at Larry, because it was nice having my sweet girls in our bedroom, not banished like they usually were to the TV room — Larry having firm rules about where youngsters belonged and when — to amuse themselves until they were called. Looking at vinyl samples, Amy knew her mind and tried to talk the other two into agreeing with her. Although I was finding it awkward to look Larry straight in the eye, I did glance over at him in the wing chair, favourite mug in hand, and caught him grinning with pleasure, watching them. It chilled my heart suddenly, because I couldn't trust anything any more, in a worse way than before. Before, it was just me suspecting, driving myself crazy.

Finally I shooed the two little ones to the TV room and Amy to the kitchen to get started on pancakes. I needed to talk. I started to pile the sample books on the floor, and he sprang from his chair to help, a sheepish expression on his face. "I'm sorry for the drinking yesterday. I wasn't in good condition to be at the wheel. I could have hurt you," he said. "I've had a lot of pressure lately at the store, but, hey, that's no excuse."

I went into the dressing room to get my thoughts together and pulled off my pretty flannel nightie and put on a pair of slacks. He was looking out the bay window, at the view that goes forever down the lake, past the island where we and the Harkers used to have picnics in the old days. The kids, what of them there were, in droopy diapers splashing in the water.

The TV was playing a "Leave It to Beaver" rerun and I could hear Amy banging the spoon against the mixing bowl. I looked at my hands and thought hard before I spoke. I told him bluntly what Bet had seen.

He drew back his head. "Say again?"

I repeated myself. It did sound off-the-wall in the light of day. Larry made a face. "And you believed her?"

"Well, yes, I did," I said, and taking a breath, added, "I've been wondering myself...if there's not something to it."

"Something to what? What are you talking about? Hey, babe. This is us here, the original home team, eh?" He shook his head and put the cup carefully on the dresser, on the doily so it wouldn't mar the wood. "My God," he said. I could hear him sigh across the room. "Oh, brother." He turned away from me again, rubbed his hands over his face and through his hair before turning back. "Look at it this way. You don't think your pal might be, uh, envious of you? That she might do anything to discredit us and our family and our success? Come on, think about it.

What has she got? And what's the big deal, anyway, about a fatherly kiss? If there was one. Why are you bothering with this? I don't mean to be, you know, offensive, but hey, is it menopause?"

He was taking his time, speaking in a reasonable tone, not defensive as I'd expected he'd be. There was something to what he said about Bet, I was aware of it, her envy. And other things. Like I'd got her a lamb's-wool cardigan last Christmas, on sale at The Bay. It was tatty-looking now, she didn't know how to maintain nice things, its royal blue faded to a smouldering-looking grey. I'd seen her wear it over a print blouse shrunk a size too small for her. And she was always in baggy jeans, she goes around deliberately looking sloppy, she doesn't have to look as plain as she does. I'd been thinking about Bet along those lines myself. The town was changing, a lot more city people coming in. No wonder they were having trouble at their funky resort. All this tumbled through my mind while I was listening, him standing so far away; and I did feel crazy, for one instant completely around the bend, as though a horribly heavy cloud had been over me for a long time, as though he was right, it was menopause, and I'd been hysterical for months. I laughed, a little sheepish myself.

Larry grinned. "Come on, let's see how our cook's doing." He walked over, wrapped his arm around my shoulders and squeezed. I was relieved. It felt better than normal.

Towards the end of breakfast — it was an afternoon-only first day of school — while we were still sitting around the kitchen table, Karen came home. She glanced into the kitchen, without a word went to shower and change. Larry mimed her holier-than-thou manner, making Jane, our giggly one, break up. I had to smile too. It was so seldom Larry had fun with the kids, I enjoyed it.

But things have a way of rearing their ugly heads. And Bet Harker's was one of them. By the next day, after the girls had had lunch and left again for school, she was phoning. At first I let the machine pick up the call. I felt shaky, like a flu was working its way into my system. Moments later she called again. "You're there, Nan, I know you're there. Pick up the damn phone."

"What?" I demanded. "I have a terrible cold as you can hear and I'd like to have a lie down before getting dinner."

"You know what's going on," she said. "She's a *kid*, Nan, she needs protecting. There, I've said it."

"You are just so determined, aren't you, to wreak havoc in my life. What is the matter with you? How do I know what you saw?" I knew there wasn't a way in the world Bet would understand it was not *him* but *them*; I knew it took two to tango in this case because of how Karen was. And then I told Bet I was going to hang up and I did. Puffing, my heart beating a mile a minute. I unplugged the phones, ran through the house doing it, feeling preyed upon.

I sent the younger ones out for ice-cream cones when Karen came home from school. I called her into the dining room, the room where I felt most at home, amidst my parents' furniture and knick-knacks. I was sitting at the table, my legs crossed, a cup of tea by my side, dosed up on Contac-C. I had on make-up, as well; I'd worked hard getting ready for this little confrontation. Karen was her usual self, cocky and arrogant, and she wouldn't sit but rested one hip against the buffet. "I want you to stop whatever you're doing with your dad," I blurted. "The flirting with him, I mean." My eyes began filling with tears. "It's the behaviour of a slut." And then she began to smile and I felt her malice like a physical thing between us and yet I couldn't prevent the tears, I let them go but did not disgrace myself by attempting to hide my face.

"Okay, Nan," she said, a shrug of one shoulder. It still bothered me, her calling us by our first names, a habit she'd started a few years back. "Slut to slut, it takes one to know one, eh? And he isn't my real dad, anyway." Giving me a look of infinite pity, she added on the way out, "So, hey, it doesn't matter, does it?"

She was an evil girl was how I felt, and I was seething with anger and drowning both, my whole life trash in polluted waters. Who was to blame for her knowing? Bet, going behind my back? And then Larry flashed into my mind and I thought, yes, he might have used that with her, "I'm not your real dad," oh, God, would he have — ? I started coughing and carried on until I was heaving, my head in the toilet bowl, and through the door Amy asking after me, and Laura, our worry-wart, starting to whimper.

Thursday afternoon Bet had the gall to knock at the door and I answered it, without thinking, wearing an apron, in the middle of deliberately doing something routine and calming, making apple pies for freezing. I didn't invite her inside, although I could tell she expected it. "If you don't take care of this situation, I'm going to talk to Boris. And I mean it." Boris Malenko was head of the Christian school we sent Karen to and he was, as well, the unofficial town counsellor. Having dropped her little bomb, Bet nodded and left. She was driving the truck with the noisy muffler.

I turned off the kitchen radio so I could think and went back to the pies, working methodically, feeling cold and righteous myself. I knew her. She was like a bulldog when she got on the case of something. If she'd already thought of going to Boris, then she was not going to give us any peace. God, I hated her then, hated her short little stubby body, her earnest little pink-cheeked face. You could know somebody and be friends — best friends — for half your life and never really know them. And while I was hating her, the very real fear of what she could do to us, how she could ruin everything I cared about, was sticking in my gut like the dough between my fingers. I had been alone in the trenches, at work protecting my family, for too long to lose it all now.

By the time Larry came home, a prime rib roast for just the two of us was in the oven and a nice bottle of red wine to go with it was open on the table. I had on a little black dress he liked. The candles were lit. I had sent the girls, including Karen, over to Mrs. Lepine's right after their dinner.

Over the last of the wine, I went over things step by step, outlined Bet's attitude and the trouble it would be for all of us, for his business, too, if anything got out, right

or wrong. Look at those nursery school teachers in Sas-
katchewan, I reminded him. Or that poor woman down in
one of the Carolinas. He wasn't as patient towards the situation as he'd been earlier in the week. "Aw, Christ, can't
that broad give it a rest," he said. "The girl's sixteen fucking years old." My face must have done something, I knew
I was wincing inside, because he reached over, patted my
hand. "Hey, babe. You and me, eh? Would I do anything
to jeopardize all we got here? God almighty." He went on
for a bit, grumbling, shaking his head.

I waited. Then I told him the plan: we had to leave for
a few days. Pull the girls out of school, send Karen down
to Rita Lee's — yes, I insisted, we had to hold our ground
with this and the way to do it was remove Bet's ammuni-
tion — send Karen to my sister's in California, the change
would do her good. The rest of us would go to Vancouver
— wasn't there a trade show he could look in on? — and
visit his mother in Burnaby, who was ailing. "The retirement home phoned just today, as a matter of fact. Got it?"

My face was flushed from the wine and from spouting
my ideas. Larry was watching me with admiration. A couple of times he snorted and nodded. "It'll blow over then,
eh," he said.

I added, "Karen might stay there, go to school?" He gave
me a sharp look but nothing more. He was hunched over,
elbows on his knees, looking forlorn. He was just a man,
plain and simple, after all, and he knew Karen wasn't his
real daughter. If he teased her — once when he was drinking too much, I saw him run his hands over her budding

breasts — and did the other things, the fooling around, looking her up and down, all those things I'd noticed, yes, but I suppose he thought, if he gave it a thought at all, thinking things through not being his forte, that what was good enough for Woody Allen was good enough for Larry Carmichael. I said, "The town's small." He sat with his thoughts for a long time. I waited.

He looked up, his eyes red-rimmed. "All right. Make the plans." He took out his gold VISA card, handed it to me. Then he rose and went for the bottle of Glenfiddich in the liquor cabinet. He poured us straight shots, raised his in a silent toast.

Bet Harker

DUST, DIRT, POTHOLES. You could make a song about Ruth, put a catchy tune to it: we got dust, we got dirt, we got potholes. Get an Italian to sing it. Council is not interested in the condition of the road up by Cedar Hideaway: "You're off the beaten track, Mrs. Harker," Boris Malenko says, shoving his glasses up his dollop of a nose. Enjoying the opportunity of jabbing back at me after our go-round last week. I stay put in the upholstered chair at the end of the council table. I admire the council chamber's high ceilings, the tall narrow windows, walls layered in dark, rich mahogany. The room has a pleasantly musty, staid smell of old paper and oak filing cabinets.

The other aldermen, there are nine, all men, shift in their seats like their hemorrhoids are pinching. They're wearing suits, those that have them; Cooey, the machine shop owner, who keeps a couple of potbelly pigs for pets, is in a fresh-pressed cotton shirt, no buttons missing.

Sam Hill from the Zoo Café has a rash on his dome that he gives a scratch, looks up from the papers piled in front of him. "Listen, we got other agenda now, Bet. It's not bothering you this time of year, the road'll be plowed up your way come winter and that's a promise. We have the FunFest to put our minds to and you give Clarence our regards and we'll be putting your request top of the list come spring."

I've heard this one before. "We're a business, we pay our taxes. I was here last spring, Sam, a lot of good it did me."

Now their papers are really rustling and there is some coughing from the gallery behind me. I'm not in the best mood; a tooth is acting up. I didn't really expect them to prioritize our road — that's the word Boris used earlier, "prioritize"; it's September, and except for flurry over this coming Fall FunFest weekend, the tourist season is over. Partly I am just acting on the squeaky-wheel theory.

Fact is, I wanted to see Boris again, to smooth over my impulsive visit to his office where I'd managed to get on his wrong side. He's smarmy, but you didn't want him for an enemy the way I look at it; he's got his finger in every pie in town. Besides being principal of the Christian school and an alderman, he's got his wife managing the new Frances Hill Retirement Home, on land donated by Sam to honour his mother, the Hills being one of Ruth's original mining families. I was late for the appointment with Boris — Clarence finally getting around to changing the oil in the truck. I arrived out of breath, skirt stuck to my thighs, hair limp, a few pine needles in it I saw afterwards, from my being caught in one of those passing downpours and standing under a tree.

I didn't want to mention Karen — my showing Nan that I was serious didn't extend to hurting her girl. To Boris I introduced a hypothetical case: If there was child abuse going on in a home, what is the procedure? He was silent, which is unnerving; silence in a conversation begs me to fill it with any words I can think of. I came up with various hypothetical situations, and he, behind his big oak desk, kept polishing his gold-rimmed glasses, replacing them, peering at me. I related a story I'd read in *Chatelaine* about a girl and her father, then bit my tongue. A bell rang, kids thudded through the halls. He leaned confidentially towards me, and said, "That's distressing news when a girl in our little town —" He let the rest hang, considered a moment, lowered his voice. "Now, just between you and me, Mrs. Harker, to make it easier on you —" and named a few names, watching me thoughtfully between each one. I thought it a breach of confidence for him to reveal names of families he knew were having trouble and I told him so.

Council has its knickers in knots about the dozen or so items on the agenda, including finding boys for the weekend parking patrol to handle all the people who will drive in for a day. It's Wednesday night before our annual Fall FunFest, and the Boy Scouts, who usually organize the parking, backed out, some flare-up between the scoutmaster, Akersly, and the FunFest Coordinator, a newcomer, a woman from the city used to hired people, not volunteers. So I heard. And on the agenda, I notice that Matthew Fauler out at Road's End Resort has some concern about the location of the soapbox derby. Cedar Hideaway isn't sponsoring an event this year; no money, no will. But I did volunteer to run the Pancake Breakfast on Saturday morning, a field-trip fund raiser for the Lake

District Highschool grade elevens, where my girl Bethany is this year.

"All right, gentlemen," I say, standing. "Your word, then, eh Sam?" I have to hold my shirt over the stretch waistband of my slacks because I can tell the waistband has rolled; some people have style and then there's me. The clerk calls the next petitioner, one of the new people from the development on Ridge Road. I don't know what's wrong out that way, a property-line dispute of some kind, but Council is in for a late night; the fellow has a thick sheaf of papers tied in ribbon.

It's still early when I leave, before eight o'clock. Weather, after a soggy week of intermittent rain, looks like it might hold for the weekend. I pat the old truck as I pass her flank, take the long way home, drive by the Carmichaels' to see if they're back. It's unlikely; they didn't leave until last Friday. Flew to see Larry's sick mother was the story I heard, while Karen went to see her cousin in California. No doubt Larry will be back this Friday; he's always MC of the No-Talent Comedy Night the Chamber of Commerce puts on.

I like looking at Nan's house, especially when nobody's around to see me drool. It's posh on the outside, Cape Cod blue aluminum siding, a side porch that overlooks the creek, a back porch facing the lake, windows everywhere. Years ago Larry rammed the tiny subdivision — four houses — through Council himself, buying municipal property cheap when Council needed money, to get his view of the lake. Tooth sparking, I turn the ignition, head home.

Clarence and the boys are in the shed, light bulb burning, not up to anything practical — like framing the new window that arrived for the campground biffy — no, they're poking through plastic trays, reacquainting themselves with fishing lures from last year, getting ready for the annual fish-in, the Father-Son FunFest Fly-Fishing Derby on Saturday. They try every year, snag lines, never win a prize. Jay finally glances over, the other two grunt. "This here one's a beauty," Clarence says, holding what looks like a hairy bug with wings. "Remember this one, how she twirled?" Clarence has a talent for being oblivious when it suits him. There they are — narrow backs in a row, each in an old flannel shirt that has never come into even remote contact with an ironing board. Jay and Jerry are Clarence's height: gangly, clumsy boys, good hearts even if they can't string together a dozen coherent words. Besides the flannel shirts, the three have on baggy jeans draping their stork legs. Jerry wears sandals, his hunky feet tough as elephant hide and impervious to cold; Clarence his year-round boots, laces untied, that I suppose one day he'll die in; on Jay a pair of ratty high-top runners. The boys inherited Clarence's run-amok hair, the kind that sticks out no matter how I cut it. One of them murmurs something, and I want to know what. But I don't ask. My hanging around, they'll just figure I'm after them for some chore.

I stand in the dirt and weed patch that passes for the yard, take a breath. I'm on my own with the situation with Nan, as I've been with everything else. It's always between us, Clarence not being able to stand real life. He cries when the kids are sick, he trembles if snow plummets off the roof. I guess he drinks to feel no pain. At times a man like that seems like no man at all.

I left Nan alone on the Tuesday after the cruise, gave her a chance to reconsider how much she knew. Worried about her because Larry was hard to deal with at the best of times, his charm the kind that deliberately undermined the other person. She kowtowed to him, always had, never got over the guilt about Karen's paternity. I pictured her in dire straits, swollen-eyed, confused by a cunning bastard who would take to lying through his capped white teeth to keep her in line. Reliving the events between us as I went about the chores, I began to give her the benefit of the doubt. She was scared — the two of us stuck on the lake as dark came on, and me moody. Until she hung up on me when I called to see how she was. Until then, I had myself convinced that really, she didn't know. I had myself convinced that given time and a chance to consider, Nan would move mountains to do the right thing.

Then when I went to her door, she opened it looking like Beaver Cleaver's mother: ruffly apron, wooden mixing spoon in hand, hair pulled neatly back. That she was not happy to see me was an understatement. When a woman looked like 1958, she was trying to make herself think there was no harm in her world. To shake her up, I threatened to tell Boris; his position as head of Karen's school would carry some weight with Nan, who cared about appearances. She shut the door on me. She didn't actually slam the door, just gazed over my head, slowly shut it. I heard the thunk of the bolt.

That was when the tooth cranked up, like it had come unwired, *pang*. A tooth on the left side of my mouth, a molar that had been teasing me with episodes of twinging. Nerves in the lower half of my jaw sprang to life. I said *OW* aloud because of the suddenness of the assault.

I'm recalling all this because on Thursday afternoon while I'm running from store to store, collecting donated goods — pancake mix, eggs, powdered milk, syrup, paper plates — I see Nan. She's standing beside her Jeep Cherokee in the parking lot of the Overweightea, talking animatedly to Fred from Century 21. Her hair is shorter and lightened, I think. She has on a two-piece green jogging suit; colourful bracelets bangle at her wrist. My heart does a silly lurch, leaping towards her — she is so familiar, so completely known to me, that my hand shoots up in a wave. Fred waves back and Nan turns, takes stock of me. I stop the cart, my heart pounding. She resumes her conversation in the same animated manner — wrists twisting, fingers flying. I am *invisible* to her.

I move forward, stunned, load the truck, drive to the Legion, where Bethany is waiting to help me unload and shelve and generally organize. She starts complaining about the heat and how long she's waited and about missing soccer practice, which we can hear coming from the downtown park. I let her complain, carry boxes inside, slam them on the counter. Stupid, caught by surprise, seeing

Nan like that. *Waving.* I wipe out the cupboards with a grungy rag, dry them with an old towel hanging on the back of a chair. Tomorrow is a Professional Development day — no school — and the team of girls and I are having a practice run-through at ten to get ready for Saturday. The Polish fellow from SausageWorks will be delivering our frozen homemade sausages this afternoon; I'm calculating there'll be just enough space in the two fridges and a cooler for four hundred sausages to thaw if we pack them in right. Thinking of details, to get my mind off of Nan.

I call to Bethany, who's supposed to be hauling in the rest of the supplies, to get a move on. When she doesn't answer, I poke my head out the door. She's in the parking lot, yakking. I do a double-take. It's Larry. Pissing hell! I duck inside; if I could undo the padlock leading to the main hall, I'd escape.

"Hey, Bet," he says, sauntering up behind me. "Saw your truck. Big weekend, eh? Lots of people already in. Saw a caravan of square dancers from Prince Rupert setting up at Mitchell Creek Campground." Like this is news, eh? He's wearing sunglasses, big-deal ones apparently, because Bethany's squealing over the name on them and dancing around him clapping.

"Stop it," I say sharply. "Just stop it."

"Oh, now, Bet, it's all right. I didn't mean to interrupt." He continues talking, calm and friendly, teasing Bethany out of her sulk, chatting about his mother in Burnaby, the family's trip to Stanley Park aquarium. What bull. I can feel his tension. My head is roaring.

"Sorry I can't lend you girls a hand, fence going up at the beer garden, promised — oh, and by the way," he says, snapping his fingers, "Nan asked me to mention that Karen will be going to school on the coast this year. California too high flying, we reckoned. But, hey. Nice change for a girl her age, don't you think?" His arm is resting near my handbag, his fingers tapping the clasp in the shape of a heart. "Cute," he says about the heart, noticing the direction of my gaze. The purse is just cheap Wal-mart crap and he knows it. He grins and clasps Bethany's shoulder. "Hey, you, you'd think it was cool going to school in the big city, wouldn't you?"

"Awesome idea," says Bethany, charmed by the grin, the tan, the muscles of his bare arms, for all I know.

"No, you wouldn't," I snap. And I almost add, Take your hands off her; but instead I fling open the door of a fridge, bend as if I know what I'm looking for. The fridge stinks: a head of lettuce completely black. Jesus. I realize I'm giving him a view of my fat ass in too-tight jeans, straighten too late. He's gone.

Bethany intones, "You are becoming really strange."

The girls are hanging around outside the Legion when I arrive the next morning. They're chattering like the teenaged girls on TV, using dramatic gestures, every third word italicized — Tammi with her Kool-Aid green hair; my Bethany acting as if she doesn't know me well (she's spent the night at Tammi's); Sarah-Ann from the donut franchise family; Kimberly and Carolyn from Ridge Road.

Esmé, the Malenko girl, shows after we've begun. Mostly she dawdles around saying, "Oh, really," as though kitchen work was beneath her.

Having eaten the breakfasts in the past, my idea is to avoid oven-dried pancakes. To accomplish this — and do the eggs and sausages — we have to be as coordinated as a Scout troop on a wilderness trip. The girls and I run through the drill, imagining flipping pancakes, plopping them on plates. One sausage, two pancakes, spoonful of scrambled eggs. An assembly line, moving the plates along to the pass-through to the waitresses, not my responsibility. Working with the girls is distracting; we're pretty good at pantomiming pandemonium. The sausages arrive, we call it a day, and the girls fly off in a flock as kids do, leaving me the imaginary clean-up. Except for Esmé, who stays behind. "I need help doing the change. Tammi says I'm no good at kitchen skills, I have to do the money." She's a lumpy girl, long bangs in her face; she'll never be the belle of the ball.

"We've got someone for money," I say, picking up the garbage bag with the lettuce in it.

"Oh." She sounds sad. What the hell, eh? She can do back-up. I sigh, glance at the clock. I plan to stop at the dentist's and see if he can fit me in. I push aside syrup bottles and sit us at the table. One fridge starts rattling and then the other. I shake my purse for coins, locate a few bills and begin drilling — senior's breakfast, so much, regular breakfast, so much, five-dollar bill, count up sixty, seventy, seventy-five, a dollar. I'd done this for a lot of kids, including my own. "Bethany wants to dye her hair green, like Tammi's. I heard them talking."

I grunt, compliment her on how fast she catches on, scoop the money into my purse. You'd think schools would teach them how to count forwards, how to give change; it's so basic.

"I saw you coming out of Daddy's office."

Now she has my attention.

She shrugs. "I was being a hall monitor because I'm so responsible." A sly look blossoms on her face. "The door of daddy's office is really, like, thin." Colour rises up my neck. She's standing now, wisely making moves to get out of my sight. She blinks coyly. "Is Bethany all right?"

Talk about getting smacked.

Alistair, our dentist, is able to squeeze me in by taking a short lunch. I recline, jaw locked open while he pokes and taps. I groan when the ice touches the tooth. He tsks, brown eyes kind beneath bushy white eyebrows. "It's a bad one, Bet. I'll do the X-ray, see what we see." While he sets up, has me bite down and hold, I am thinking how my hand shook as I was locking the Legion — Clarence and Bethany indeed. Leaving the dentist's with a prescription for antibiotics, the worst of it sinks in: the idea of me being the type to tolerate such monstrous behaviour for even one second.

Clarence is trundling down the lane leading to our place, pulling a wagon with a tree lying in it, roots bundled in burlap. I stop the truck and ask him what in the world he's doing. "Planting antique apple trees. Got from Eunice's," he says. "Bulldozers at her place tomorrow."

The man is positively dim-witted. "There are a thousand things that need doing, Clarence Harker. Alistair says I need a root canal, and do you think we can afford that? No, not on your life. I bust my butt around here. For what? We can't afford dick," I say, using an expression the kids are into.

"Ah, Bet," sighs Clarence, pained. "Don't be so jealous of Nan and Larry. They have their problems too."

I gun the truck, leave him in the dust.

At six a.m. in the frigging morning as I'm opening the kitchen, Bethany in tow, I vow I will never volunteer to do anything again. Throughout the night I had diarrhea, what my kids used to call "dire-rear," caused by the antibiotics, and now a viselike headache seems to be the newest side effect. The kitchen is dark and chilly. I flick on the fluorescent lights, turn on the radio to rev us up. The other girls arrive, muttering but excited, and we're in business. By seven we hear people scraping chairs, greeting each other, and soon we're knee deep in fried sausages and runny pancakes. The grade twelve girls, serving at the breakfast in exchange for the elevens serving at their end-of-year Parent-Teacher Tea, tap long fingernails, impatient for their orders. Paper plates full of food land on the floor occasionally. We kick the contents aside, step in grease, keep going. The action takes my mind off the headache.

Towards the end — breakfast is from seven to nine —

Bethany gives Esmé a push and she loses her balance, skids onto the floor. I command the others to keep working, go to her aid, take the two girls by the arm into the parking lot. People are smoking out there, and I nod pleasantly to this one and that one and pull the girls around the side of the building. "For frigging sakes," I hiss at Bethany. "What is this?"

"Mummy, Esmé is saying horrible, disgusting things about Daddy." There are tears in her eyes.

I gawk at Esmé. She flicks her eyes triumphantly is how I read it, then lowers them, mouth twitching. It's appalling what the Malenko family thinks it can get away with in this town — they've even got some relative who's mental tucked away in the Frances Hill — and I've had it up to here. "You brat." My hand slaps her on her bare upper arm. Not hard, just enough to reverberate, in time, all over town. I sense it even before I feel the satisfying, stinging impact of my hand against her solid flesh, before she goes running off in a high-pitched wail. I lost it, I will say to the court of the community. I had a toothache that made me crazy and then there were the antibiotics. How else could I explain striking a kid? It will be shocking, the sin-filled revelations we will all hear about me, in due course.

"God, you're so temperamental," Bethany says. "I didn't mean for you to *attack* her." There's awe in her tone. But I lean back against the wire fence, feeling out of control.

From the dinghy once at twilight Nan and I saw them, last year, maybe the year before. The boys and men coming down to fish, silent as deer. We watched them emerging from the woods in twos, buddies or fathers and sons, their rubber boots, their rods, their hats, their gear in hand, and then they cast into the water, one there on the edge, his boots on shiny rocks, one there, where the creek begins to fan, one over there by a logjam, up to his calves. They separated themselves like sportsmen and gentlemen, giving one another room to whip a line back over a shoulder, zing it out, reel in.

In the beer parlour afterwards, they wouldn't be gentlemen, some of them, that was for sure; they would be rowdy and rough. But there in the twilight, the water still as a summer noon, colours deepening from blues to inky greys, the moon not yet over the mountains, the sun entirely gone from the pass it catches itself on at that time of year, I remember longing for something, I remember being sad about the ordinariness of life, I guess. I didn't know, then, that there would come a time when I wouldn't have my closest friend any more, that Larry would grow distant and Clarence never understand why, that the kids would lose people they thought were family. Ordinary is maybe *it*, it's what we should be grateful for.

"Now, Mum," Bethany says and pats my hand. It's dusk, she and I on the point, perched on a log, watching the distant clusters of fathers and sons assemble around the creek mouth for the start of the derby. We're not alone, people are sitting quietly, shooing the occasional fly. It's been a long day. Across the bay we see beach fires and hear the sounds of laughter. Music echoes from the new teen centre, just far enough away to suit me. Bethany says, "Now, Mum. Everybody behaves dumb sometimes. It's the human condition, you know?"

I reach over, give her leg a squeeze. Larry saying, "You don't turn me on, Bet, you just don't." Me seventeen, dumb as they come. And it's just as well, when I think about it. In my men there is a harmlessness that I guess I can be thankful for. I think of Clarence's hands, not half bad: big hands, long, shapely fingers and curved-back thumbs.

"It's not the end of the world," Bethany pipes up, ever helpful.

"Bethany."

I hear her mutter, "Oh, all right," in the falling light, followed by a long, ragged "I tried" exhale. I'm thinking of how those men in the twilight between-time were different from what women see. Nan and I had whispered about it. The silence in them had caught us by surprise, the silence and the nearness of grace. My tooth gives a resilient whang. God, I am looking forward to pulling the bugger out with pliers. I wonder if it's possible that even my Clarence has a deep side to him. Doubt it. But he might know where a pair of pliers are, he might be good for that.

ALGORITHMS

Rita Lee Wanaker

I FIND MYSELF AT TWILIGHT perched on the roof of my house in the foothills of Santa Barbara, perched like a stuffed owl on the one flat section, holding Walrus, my beloved old English pug, who is drugged and dying, and overhead are a few stars and at Millie and Russ's house across the field car doors slam and now the horse is heard from, fleabag Gardenia snorting and thumping the dirt in her paddock. I am dizzy from excess and lack — lack of sleep, lack of food, from too much sun, too much daughter, from the wild, burnt-honey grasses in the field for too long rising like tinder, a blaze in the making, and I'm wishing, don't we all, that I could simply catch fire and *get it the hell over with.*

It is the end of September and I have stood everything long enough. Yesterday morning, I think it was yesterday, over a gin and lemonade I became tired of arguing with Everett on the phone, from Boston, I think, some conference, who was saying, "My God, you know Walrus is disgusting. Get with the program, dearheart. Do something about the damn dog before I get back." And while I pity Walrus, I won't take him to the vet to be put down, which is what Everett wants, the fighting going on between us through the dog, who is blind and nearly deaf and then diarrhea and the rest of it. But in his house — our house — what is tacitly mine is the dog, and Everett won't interfere, although he is a man of action, as he said twenty years ago when I was being courted by him, a handsome older man, at a time when his pronouncements were not pompous but defining and thrilling — they had the power to invent reality — and in the old cabin outside the town of Ruth, us on the braided rug: "I am a man of action, Rita Lee."

His daughter Rosalind, Rozzy, the one child of ours, the not-the-boy-Ev-wanted child of ours, is a girl of action, too, these days, slamming out of the house half the time, tip-toeing out the other, confusing the issue that is actually going on, which is her deliberate throwing up. She runs from me, this girl, avoiding contact. Only does this garbage behaviour for my benefit, not when her father's at home, so I don't know how to bring it up — no pun intended — with him. I don't know how she's going to graduate; over the summer she got worse and I think she doesn't bother to go to school some days. I am so angry at her I could shake her silly. This is supposed to be the year of the social whirls, the fun things.

Shagged breathing, soot in my throat from the fires down the coast. The field grasses are dangerously tall — I see a swath through them where last night Roz waded out to water her horse. The heat started at the end of May, con-tinued through the summer, into the fall, killing everything, depressing the usually cheery eucalyptus trees, their leaves that the slightest breeze causes to flutter instead merely dangling, dispirited. The temperature hovers around one hundred degrees in the shade and water is scarce, burping out of the tap in reluctant trickles, especially in the evening when demand is high. I'm not demanding. I haven't turned the dishwasher on in a week. Everett's been away six days, is due back tonight or tomorrow, he doesn't say lately, and I don't care. My arm aches — bursitis, arthritis — from the weight of Walrus, drooling and snoring, pink-tipped tongue protruding. Grey bristly hairs, his whole body a beard of them. He dribbles from his ass, poor fellow, and is stalwart when I clean him up. In his dotage he has laid claim to being in the world through his relationship to air: he stinks it up, he fills it with farts and grunts. I could end him in a whump: release the tension in my back and arm and let him bump across the welts of fired clay and over the edge with ye, matey. Into what was the herb garden before the drought. He has been cooperative and trusting, swallowed every pill I've mashed for him. I shift, roll Walrus tighter into his filthy little rug.

Roz left without a word this morning. I heard her little Honda whine out of the driveway. I swallowed a .5-mg lorazepam for anxiety, went down and met the kitchen for the first time since yesterday noon. Found bits of food everywhere, soggy packages of defrosted lima beans, corn, peas pooling on the counter. Everywhere, evidence of Rozzy, her show-not-tell statements, and me hiding like a chickenshit in my locked room, listening to her goings-on. At the stuff on the floor beside the work island I stared, momentarily flummoxed. There were opened containers, five cans and a microwavable food package: applesauce, rice pudding, creamed corn, corned beef hash, ravioli, macaroni and cheese. "Christ," I said aloud. *In a row*.

They ate soft things, the therapist told me. I consulted with somebody out of town, a specialist down in Ventura. I used a fake name. Soft foods, said the therapist, were easier on the throat when regurgitating. Everett will despise me. Half-eaten bits of this and that. He has a busy, important life; in his spare time, outside the hospital, besides his research project, he's editing a collection of essays about the psychological factors in gynecological illnesses.

In June, the morning after I found the closet mess, she was standing over the sink, ready for school. I hadn't slept until dawn, then overslept. Seeing her there as I entered the kitchen caused a flip-flop in my heart.

She made a half-turn towards me and I saw she was into a cantaloupe, nibbling quarter-moons, wearing a dish-towel bib. She was dressed for school, white blouse and jeans, looking wholesome and neat, her beautiful brunette hair up in a French roll. I thought, seeing her so perfect like that, even if she is big-boned like Everett, that maybe it was me who was off, maybe I'd imagined all the slop. When she is herself, Roz has a thing about neatness.

I wanted to confront her. Tell me about the half-eaten Hershey bars. The opened bags of now-stale taco chips.

Did you have a party in your room, maybe some night while I was away? I coughed.

"Everything okay with you?" I finally choked out, sat at the table, holding my chin, trying to look friendly and unconcerned. These days I had to be careful around her, everything I said was misconstrued. And really, what was I wanting to find out? Have you barfed in public lately? Does anybody know? "You look good."

She shot me a look. She has a haughty manner that can be intimidating. "Yeah, right."

"Well, you do."

"Lame, Mom. See you." She swooped her backpack off the counter. I heard her car start, the little red Honda Ev surprised her (and me) with when she passed her driver's exam.

Quality time.

Awake. Heard her again, her innards plummeting into the bowl.

There was a moment when I screwed up my courage and knocked and entered Ev's study to ask how the book was going and could I make him some coffee. We sipped it standing at the counter that looks out on the field and at Gardenia's paddock along the far wall, where Millie and Russ's place starts. It was already too hot, too dry. "No rain yet," Ev said, then glanced pointedly — he is always so pointed about it — at his watch.

My heart was flipping as though I'd raced around a

track. Now. Now, I thought. Take him to her room and show him your discovery.

He said, "Oh, Christ. I forgot about the damn consultation. See you, dearheart."

See you, dearheart.

See you.

Blew it. I lose courage with every opportunity I let pass.

Thinking about the little cabin in Ruth, how the wind from the lake found its way through the flimsy windows, how they rattled at night in a storm. The windows were ripply, the world distorted through them, but in a comforting way: you knew it was the ancient glass causing it. I'd given up drugs when I married Everett; didn't seem right, a stoned doctor's wife, although I know now there are enough of them; their drugs are legal, is all.

We were in Ruth that fall, Everett meeting the family, my sister Nan's husband, Larry, giving us the use of his family's cabin for a week. Maybe Ev and I should have stayed in Ruth, flowed with the seasons of the mountains and the lake, the tides of life in my home town — the church teas and school bazaars, the autumn canning, the summer corn feeds — our child growing strong and healthy. And I would have had flower baskets hanging along the porch of our modest house and every morning carried the stool out, to stand on in order to water each basket full of lobelia, pansies, petunias, ageratum, geraniums, delighting in the play of pinks and blues and purples as I picked off dead flowers, tossed them over the railing into the tiger lilies —

I would have had many varieties of tiger lilies — and carrying the stool from basket to basket, refilling the watering can from the spigot at the side of the house, down and up I would have gone, taking time to breathe in the fresh air, admire the sky, the rim of mountains we would have seen from our house, the play of light on them.

Ev saying, "Aren't you glad you didn't marry the hang glider?" We were packing then, he tossing things into the bags willy-nilly. He meant because he found Ruth so limited, my family boring. He was in a hurry to get back to Seattle, where we were living then. He had a position in a new clinic and we lived in a rented house with a damp basement. It rained every day.

The hang glider turned into a womanizer, so Nan put it. Still flying, though.

The kitchen is sweltering, but I don't turn on the air conditioning, I need the build-up of heat in my body, the full-to-the-brim bursting faintness I experience just before my pores release the perspiration down my nose, the bony space around my breasts. Withstanding this heat feels like worthwhile exertion, involving me in more than the mere saving of kilowatts; for the moment I can resist hopping in the Cherokee and driving out for booze. I can bear up under Roz's siege. I can leap into the unknown; I've done it. Jumped off a mountain, been carried by wind. A tandem flight. I knew I was going to leave Ruth, even then.

At last I decide it's time. I set the can of chili I've been eating from in the refrigerator and go to the pantry to collect Walrus where I've stored him for the last while and then I lug him up the stairs to the master bedroom and from there I spiral up the narrow staircase to the roof blanketed by heat that won't quit even as dark comes on and the sun, orange as poison, is down. He might have convulsions or barf on me or shit on me, I don't care, I want the torment over with. I see the first star.

Ev did not want to hear about an old woman's breasts when I tried to tell him about my ridiculous conference with Rozzy's teacher. He was humiliated that his only child was "risking public censure" by failing kindergarten. How could anyone fail kindergarten? he wanted to know. I think I said she didn't belong in his fancy private school, she would have been happier in a public one. I don't know. Maybe I didn't open my mouth.

I wonder why I involved him at all. I separated myself from his anger, yet enjoyed it, watched his tongue busily poking the inside of his cheek, passing across his front teeth to the other side of his mouth, repeating the probing there, an unconscious habit. It was like the "mousy cleaning the housy" game I'd learned in grade two: the tongue was a broom cleaning first the right inner cheek, then the left, cleaning the ceiling, then the floor and finally, finally — this was the part Rozzy and her friends loved — brushing the dirt right out the door.

For Everett, the fact that the children of our friends were doing fine was the clincher. (Millie and Russ had bought the next piece of property by then, and started on their swimming pool.) Other people's kids doing fine was the crux of it, or the beginning of it — the lessons, the badgering, the tears, after dinner and Saturday mornings, Ev "teaching" our little Rozzy, using jars of my homemade preserves or pickled beets, his white shirtsleeves rolled to the elbow, the older father being casually no-nonsense: "How many jars of jam do we have here, honey? Two, that's right. And now, how many jars of jam do we have, honey? Three, that's a good girl, that's Daddy's good girl. Three. Now. Daddy takes away and puts behind his back one jar of jam and how many are left, honey?"

And Rozzy would shout triumphantly, "Three! Because you still have the other jar, Daddy, you can't fool me!"

I loved her then, that innocently aggressive spirit wearing him down.

Went for the endoscopy in August. Everett set up the appointment with Dr J., the "best" (of course). Body falling apart with stress. An ulcer this time. Everybody very nice, complimenting me on my bravery, as though I were a child, because I wouldn't let them knock me out with a Valium-related drug that made me feel hit by a hammer — wake from it in a horrible state of vertigo, nauseated and fighting. In a sweat Arrid Extra Dry was not going to stop as Dr. J. gave my throat a local, I lay on my side on the table, breathing slowly, rhythmically — all the exercises I have learned from being coerced into going to Millie's various New Age events; departing from my body, lifting off, so that I won't move and gag and suffocate as he snakes the coil past my open mouth, down my open throat into my stomach, where he peers around for the ulcer. The nurse murmuring to me what a good job I'm doing, ready I'm sure at any second to stab me with a knockout drug should I flinch. My eyes closed, as close to being without thought as I am capable of, aware of this metal thing in me, feeling the dullness of it probing the length of my torso and a weird sickening emptiness in my stomach. "Fine," he says. "Great. Just a moment more. Wow. Beauty."

Love it when they're into their work.

Prescribes Losec, a new drug to heal the volcano in the duodenum. No more Voltaren for arthritis. I start to panic, how can I survive without it? He suggests Tylenol for a while. Ulcers are where it's at. Everett thinks arthritis is psychosomatic.

At first, I assumed Roz's cache of food was for a sleep-over or a camp-out — which was ridiculous, she never did those things, but I wanted the stashed food to make some sense. What had brought me into her room? Some ordinary, housewifely, motherly reason. What made me open the closet door, check the shelves, search under piles of unwashed clothes? Didn't know, mind a blank. Saw the jars of applesauce and lunch-pack-sized cans of tapioca, dozens of mauled-looking, partly chewed candy bars. Browsed through smelly plastic bags, mouldy scraps of pizza crusts, bemused. What I was beholding was so *absurd*: we had plenty of food in the kitchen, another freezer in the basement.

Carefully, almost tenderly, I put everything back where I found it, went downstairs and lifted the lid of the chicken Cacciatore I was simmering and let the steam swirl over my face and put the lid back on the pot and looked out the window and hated Gardenia more than usual — she was a mean, conniving creature whenever I was around, always had been. But giving a girl a horse was supposed to ensure normal development, it was axiomatic, and Gardenia had *failed,* it wasn't like she had other things on her mind, for God's sake, she wasn't a racehorse or a pacer or a trotter, she was a *family* horse who stayed at home. Her job specs were simple: give love, be pretty, entertain.

After she leaves for school I stand outside her room and look in. Her room is so pretty, the girl's room Nan and I always wanted, ruffled canopy above the bed, burgundy and pink flowered wallpaper. In my chest, a panicky feeling where the opening for the heart chakra is — like hell, Millie, I want to shout: chakra, shmakra — where love, Millie assured me, flows from. The whole thing with Roz a can of worms, best not opened.

I've had Walrus since he was born, the year Rozzy was five and midway through kindergarten, the time the teacher called me in to discuss Rozzy's "learning problem": she couldn't add and subtract objects to ten. Mrs. Worth — ironic name — wasn't kind about Rozzy's inability to move ice-cream sticks from one place to another, to demonstrate her understanding of basic algorithms. Made me sit at a little table in the Cozy Corner, knees practically to my chin. I reminded her that Rozzy was a young five, a fall birthday. I was never a crackerjack student and thought I had to be nice to teachers so they wouldn't be mean to my child. Mrs. W. went through the process of using the ice-cream sticks so I would understand — how patronizing, and me sitting there respectfully, letting her do it. Stooping, showing me, she exuded layers of intricate smells, mostly onion and lilac water. I remember the hair on her scalp, bone-white a quarter-inch along the part. I was mesmerized by the massive, wrinkly breasts quivering inside the scoop-necked dress. I thought those breasts would traumatize little boys.

Millie is dealing with mid-life by getting into New Age this and that. Changes on a "cellular" level are big just now. For a moderate fee, Millie will lead you through a "rebirthing" and then you'll feel better on a cellular level. Gin makes me feel better on a cellular level, but Millie doesn't like to hear it.

Walrus got so he wouldn't go outside, even if I carried him. The heat and sunshine made him shiver and he wound himself in anxious circles. This morning he raised his head in recognition at the sound of my sandals on the stairs leading to the root cellar, the only place he is comfortable in the whole house. His sleepy stub of a tail barely twitched in greeting. As the afternoon slips away, I feed him mashed drugs in fingerfuls of his favourite liver, acutely aware that he is losing touch with parts of himself.

Rozzy was five years old that summer in Tahoe. No, four still, almost five, the summer before that dreadful kindergarten year. Everett was teaching her to dive. I was treading water, watching the two of them on the raft. Thunderheads were forming above the mountains, ominous billows of them. All the other families, sensibly fearing lightning, had gone in. Everett said, "Oh for Christ's sake." His voice ricocheted off the delicious, licorice-colour water. I called over, "Go on, pumpkin, Daddy knows, *just do it.*"

Rozzy's teeth were chattering. She giggled, trying to be appealing, to be cute. She was a big-boned girl even then. Her flirting annoyed Everett, I know, annoyed him because she wasn't cute or especially pretty. "Please, Daddy," she said. She skittered back to the safe centre of the raft. He frowned at her. She ran flinging her arms towards the edge, brought her compact body to a stricken halt. "I can't. I'm scared, I can't." I was paddling this way and that, up to my neck in cold water.

I saw his hand draw back and start towards her. I shivered at a passing breeze ruffling the water. He said, "I wish to God you'd been a boy." And then she was flying, her face alive with surprise and fear.

I didn't see it. I didn't see him batting her bottom. A thunderclap drew my attention to the mountains behind me, and I know I was looking away. I came up with things:

maybe he didn't hit her, maybe she lost her balance, jumped to compensate. I know I turned at the first crack of thunder reverberating out of the north. I missed the gesture that had swept the child choking into the lake. A sheet of rain like a blowing curtain came towards us. I let my sphincter muscle go, which took concentration. Urine created a hot bubble in the crotch of the bathing suit until it broke through and eddied around one leg and entwined my buttocks encased in nylon spandex and warmed the slick skin of my chilled thighs.

Everett will blame me. He'll work it around that it's my fault about Roz. It is, somehow, but I don't understand. I picture myself confronting him with the news, but I keep stepping backwards, falling from view. I hug Walrus's cooling body. My knee hurts, one of my many endless pains. Everett will come home full of himself from meetings and contacts. Roz will come home carrying her secrets. I won't know where she's been, what she's been up to, or with whom. It will humiliate him if it gets out about her.

From Millie's healing circle voices float across the field, staking pitches, finding harmony, holding vowels rounding into hums, the sound throbbing in the dark. They will have taken off their shoes, drunk their ginseng tea — I've been there — and holding hands, formed their circle of prayer, and into the circle of prayer placed the names of those in need, their voices murmuring a chorus of names of those in need — "Rozzy, Walrus, Rita Lee," I say to myself, joining their chanting of the sounds that blend them and make them feel like one, send their energy, so they believe, into the earth, into the universe, Millie wearing her Mexican silver-and-abalone cresting-moon earrings, her house tilting on its axis and revolving, lit up like a spaceship. Delicate lapping of water, Gardenia drinking from her big metal tub, stars softening, blurring at their edges, and the tree frogs and the crickets chirrup and in the distance faint breathing that is actually close, when I think, at last, to tilt my head and press an ear to Walrus's nostrils, and listen. The silky sound of his breath is so unlike his usual, it's as though he has already transcended, caught the wind, come out of himself and moved on.

Rozzy Wanaker

I DON'T KNOW what she thought sitting on the roof watching the humongous fire heading her way, she must have thought she deserved it, I mean, she had a massive guilt always eating at her, you could tell, she was so distracted sometimes and angry, she was always angry at Daddy for something. And at me, although I don't know how true that really is. About me she had conflicts, the counsellor who talked to me said. I mean, here I was, a fairly cool girl — oh, bag it. I don't have one cool hair on my cretinous head and who do I think I'm bluffing? Okay, here I was, a girl, an only child and loved by Daddy, who maybe loved me more than her, the counsellor said, but she had never lived inside the walls of our "compound," what Daddy, who was raised partly in Indonesia, called our house.

The house — the Wanaker house, ours — was, like, surreal. They both needed it: the unusual architecture, the view, the sunsets, the gin martinis, the pool, the basic Mexican layout. The house faced in on itself, with a few additions like outcroppings, the balcony across the front for the ocean view, the flat-roof section because Rita Lee wanted to camp under the stars. The basic inward looking was a big mistake, because that left the three of us studying each other, which was lame to the extreme. We needed

more children in our family, I think, then the pressure
would have got off me and I might have turned out better
and Rita Lee, Mom, less neurotic about being a housewife
who had one daughter and that daughter bulimic and
barfing everywhere in sight and out of sight, a stage I
haven't entirely yet grown out of, although Daddy, now
that he found out about it, has me seeing "a new man," a
psychiatrist who specializes in problem cases, which Daddy
sees me as. Daddy is a gynecologist but doesn't get his
hands on the work any more — he is into theory and writing papers. I mean, how many vaginas can you look at and
poke around in and still want to get down with your wife?
No wonder Rita Lee was walking around alternately an
aggravated motor-mouth or viscerally non-verbal so much
of the time. I mean, she probably needed to, like, get it on
a regular basis.

As for me, I'm not interested in sex, which makes me
odd girl out at school. I think I might be lesbian, although
it's hard to say. I got my nose pierced and Daddy had a
conniption, he said I was underage and if I didn't tell him
who did it, he would find out and report the moron himself, but of course he never really tried; he just put some
antiseptic on it — Daddy has breath that smells of dead
garlic and I don't like it — and swore some and shook his
head, normal things for a man of his generation. And then
he did the usual, got on the phone. I listened outside the
door — we were staying in a residential suite in a hotel,
two bedrooms and an office as well as living room while
the insurance was being settled, Daddy was intent on that

insurance — sort of hoping the call would be about me, you know, like asking around who does these radical mutilations on perfectly fine specimens of humanity, but that wasn't it; he was calling his co-author on a study they were doing about the incidence of ovarian tumours in women on Provera for x number of years, or some drug, maybe it wasn't Provera. My mom was into drugs. She had a medicine cabinet full of everything you could name. She had books on details of prescription drugs, the big one that she made Daddy get her and then a bunch of others for "lay people," the general public. I guess when you look at it, Mom was sick a lot. It's not something a daughter of my type thinks much about. I mean, I knew she had arthritis, because she wore heat bands on her wrists sometimes and sometimes she stuck her feet in a heated jelly a physio had given her. And she didn't eat that much, either, because she couldn't exercise like normal women and she was afraid of getting fat, just like me, although the psychiatrist is trying to say my mother and I didn't even have that in common. He's trying to say her response to her situation was, like, healthy and mine sick and therefore I am dis-eased. When I put it that way to him, he purses his lips and tries to not look disapproving, but it's hard when you're around me, I have a talent for driving men wild in the wrong way — Daddy is a case in point. Ever since I was little he has winced when he looked at me. I know this, although when I brought it up to him once, we were hav-ing breakfast in the hotel coffee shop, and Millie, whom I've know for practically my whole life, wasn't welcome to visit us or her husband Russ either, even though Daddy and him had been friends for years. It had to do with blame but what could anybody have done to stop it anyway, with Rita Lee trapped on the roof for one thing or, for another, the horrible water pressure being what it was because the city council had put stall tactics on improvements and it was just lucky the whole section didn't go up in flames. "Thank goodness," Daddy said, "for the boys on the trucks."

Daddy was bent out of shape about Millie, because a man from Millie's taking a cigarette break from the chanting at the healing circle (Millie was into New Age big time) started the fire. The man obviously lived in an apartment, didn't know anything about grass and fire, because when Millie tinkled her bell to call them back to the house, he threw his cigarette away, just tossed a lit butt right into the field that we never bothered taking care of because Daddy was too busy and Rita Lee wouldn't get around to hiring a man to do it — she had a stubbornness that drove me and Daddy crazy — and Daddy was travelling massively during that time and so he neglected it. That's all he could say after the tragedy, "I neglected my duty, I neglected to have the field shorn." Daddy spoke that way sometimes because he was older: the field "shorn," for instance, sounded just like from the half-semester I lasted in Bible study class in tenth grade when they stuck me in it because they needed another body to make the class go. Well, the butt caught the hay in Gardenia's stall and the next thing anybody knew the wind came up from the south — the poisonous gases from L.A. — and blew the storm of fire right at our house and Rita Lee sitting on the roof, totally true, with our dog half or already dead and she didn't even try to get down or make a run for it or anything, Daddy said. And it wasn't like she was totally stoned or drunk, either, although Walrus sure was. Not drunk, but stoned out of his little scrag head on pills.

So Daddy and I were at the Paradise Hilton, on the beach in Santa Barbara, which I secretly thought was pretty cool after having had to beg rides for years from the hillside or lately drive my own little Honda down to the beach and turn into a melty before even getting to the water, well, it was okay, just prancing out of the hotel, a towel over my shoulder. It was like Hawaii without the same quantity of flowers.

Aunt Nan had already done a fly-in, fly-out. She's still living in the little town where she and Mom were born. She's trying to say I should go live there, take my cousin Karen's room because Karen is going to school in Vancouver and I would like it in Ruth and it would be a nice wholesome change for me. She's not mad anymore that Mom nixed Karen's visit; Aunt Nan likes things nice. She's kind of chirpy, except when she cries it's like an eruption that catches her by surprise. She says it's her version of a breakdown and then goes to check her make-up in a mirror, even if you're in the middle of a sentence. She's distracted like Mom and might change the subject to the bags under her eyes when she's been talking about Mom and her ice skating on a pond when they were kids. Halfway through a bottle of room-service white wine — which made me wonder if alcoholism, like distraction, runs in my mom's family, making them more millennium than I thought — she said about the bags under her eyes, "They're the weights I carry as a result of a life lived on the edge," and then she laughed her sharp little laugh. She said she would talk to Daddy about me living with them. I could envision it as being a mildly cool thing, living in Canada. You don't get so randomly shot at there. "The idea is on the back burner," Daddy mumbled at breakfast after Aunt Nan left; and by his deliberating tone, I could tell he was looking forward to it, the idea of me being gone. He was eating EggBeaters and Slender toast and chewing like it was a duty. And I said, "You never have liked me, really liked me, have you?" And he frowned, irritated, and took another crunch and shook his head, glanced down at the bacon fat and fried potatoes on my plate and winced. And I said, "See? You do that all the time. I look like you is why and I'm a girl and you're ugly."

I got out of there but still took my time, actually. Daddy is not the type to make a scene anywhere in the vicinity of another human being within half a mile. I'd had a large breakfast, the Diver's Special, just to test him. I didn't intend to keep it. I have this system where I can up-chuck by just looking at a toilet bowl at a certain angle. I'm really good at it; a couple of girls are impressed with the speed I'm in and out of a stall. Other times I need more coaxing and the finger on my throat, not in it, but pinching on the outside is signal enough; it's like there's a part of me knows that I have the perfect capability of pinching my throat until I nearly suffocate. I have that kind of power over my autonomic nervous system, a talent that no one knows about really, and if they did, wouldn't appreciate. It's hard to see it as adding practical economic value to my future life.

I have a "family" elsewhere, which is why I had been tolerating Rita Lee and Daddy. I discovered the Fourth Avenue Mission and food bank six months ago and the crowd that works there is totally dedicated to something besides their own selfishness and personal gain. Eva, who's the social worker, plans barbecues for homeless people and single mothers and she lets me help her sometimes. She let me help paint the butcher-paper banner to put in the park. Not a whole lot of people show up for Eva's barbecues, but she doesn't get discouraged. (I think people probably don't like the hymn singing but I haven't mentioned my theory yet.) They're very Christian at the food bank and when you're dealing with God and good works, you don't worry the way other people do. Except about money, they are always worried about money. I used to borrow a twenty now and then from Rita Lee's purse and she wouldn't miss it. It was my way of helping her contribute to the charity of my choice instead of to Canyon Liquors. Anyway, since the fire I've only been to the food bank once and they were surprised to see me running through the maze from office to office, happy to see them. It felt like I'd been away forever. They didn't need my help that day but I was cool with it. I went around to the back entrance and said hi to

Danusha, who was on the computer. What we do is, when people come in to get their food — they can only come to our mission once a month — the person at the computer has to look up their file and see their welfare or immigration card and mark that they were there that month, so there's no cheating. Danusha said she was sorry about my mother, how awful, I must be feeling terrible, and I said yes, it was awful; but then, leaving — people were waiting, she had work to do — I brainstormed on whether it was awful or not and it was inconclusive because I was basically numb.

It was pretty horrible right after Mom and Walrus and Gardenia died, along with every stuffed animal anybody had ever laid on me during my whole life. The thing was, just before the "immolation" — a newspaper reporter got that word into his cranium and loosed it in the paper — I had run away for a couple of days but the effect was nullified because when I came home, driving the Honda with a new dent in the fender, a back-alley escape from some Ventura dickheads in a pick-up, a part of town I shouldn't have been in, in the first place, as Rita Lee in her motherly mode would have said, there was nothing where once there had been everything. I mean, part of the structure of the garage was still available but the house was piles of burnt brick and pretty much black mush, like when I tried throwing up a few bags of half-chewed licorice — revolting. It sticks in your nose. The north-side wall was still standing, like the fire was satiated after crossing the field and consuming almost the whole house and that wall just stood up to it: You can't eat me. You could see bits of furniture and charred books even where I was, in the supposed driveway. The policeman dozing behind the wheel with an ice-cream stick still in his hand managed to catch me as I was reversing. Without knowing what I was doing, I thought I was in the wrong place; how could a whole house be gone? So he caught me and then Daddy came and we went over to the hospital in his new Chrysler, purring silently down the winding roads and Daddy's mouth working and him trying to word how to tell me. Well, it was obvious, wasn't it. Where was Rita Lee in all this? It wasn't like Mom to miss out on any thrills. I mean, she had always been seriously present when it came to disaster: she and I chased ambulances when I was little, she was fascinated by gory wreckage. In his office at the hospital, I started shaking and stuffed my hands one after the other in my mouth. I was remembering when Daddy and I came home with Gardenia on my ninth birthday, Mom was totally bent out of shape at not being told about us getting a horse. What made me sad in remembering the scene was that she wasn't a shirker, my mom. She would have figured out a solution to me eventually. She was just taking her time thinking.

I realize that I didn't *realize* sooner what had gone down as I drove up to the house because you don't pay much attention when you're coming home; it's such a common occurrence, like duh, yeah. You just let the car lead and get out thinking your own thoughts and that's as far as it goes. I should have caught on sooner to the destruction because I should have smelled it, if I'd had the windows rolled down and not the air conditioning on and the music so loud. It practically tormented me, thinking how I was so blind as I approached the house I'd grown up in, and not noticed that it wasn't there. But they say the brain takes a while to adjust to a reality hit that unexpected. Like the shock of it had me dissociated is what the shrink explained. When I rolled down the window, puzzling, I could smell the burntness of extinction, a total smell, mixed in with some chemical that I found out later the fire department mixes in with their water. There were big hunks of field-grass roots still clinging to the black soil but the rest was ashy and sooty, wet and tarry-looking.

They told me Rita Lee wouldn't have burned to death before she died. I mean, the force of the fire, the heat of it, would have killed her pretty much a hundred per cent before the flames themselves touched her. She would have been overcome by the force of the fire's heat, like on your way to hell before Beelzebub gets his claws into you. I know her body burned, they don't keep facts from kids, but they were in strategy about how she didn't suffer. Like she might have been looking away and then turned and seen the fire and her heart would have got a reflex from that fact, but then because the fire was moving so fast and the grasses were so dry, it would have sent its searing whoosh right into her nostrils and down to her lungs and that would have been that. They want me to believe it because in their motif is the concept of hellfire and they believe that's the worst thing that could happen to a person.

I'm not so sure. Plain fear is high on my list: fear of water, fear of food, now add fear of fire.

Millie had to wait until Daddy was at the hospital to come to the hotel to see me because he was pissed at her, like unreasonably. Something juvenile was going on between them is all I know. She has a comfortable shape for a woman her age, sexy, I think, round and tanned really smoothly, every crevice looked after. She wears these super earrings she gets when they travel to the desert or to Mexico; she looks cool in silver and turquoise, it goes with her dark curly hair and brown eyes. She gets off on being mistaken for a foreigner, but of course the quality of her clothes and jewellery are a dead giveaway she's not some Mexican hot across the border, no offence. But the day she snuck into the hotel and we sat by the pool drinking daiquiris in her case and Coke in mine, she was looking glum, injured and out of sorts. Her eyes were swollen from crying. She loved my mother, that was the thing. They were best friends for years, the two families of them and us had built big houses about the same time and there used to be pool parties — they had the big pool, we just had our private, in-house pool — and a lot of back and forth when we kids were growing up. I had gone to school with Deborah and Stephen, who were away at boarding school, and Millie had been wanting to ask me, should she bring them home? They were just dying there in Boston, feeling so ratched about Rita, but I said the truth, they were kids and they would get busy with other things and what could they do here anyway? And

Millie had enough respect for the situation not to tell me they would be any help to me because I never got along with her kids. They were the smart ones, techie and intellectual, the ones that made Daddy look askance at me. It wasn't my fault he married Rita Lee instead of someone smart like Millie. I read in the newspaper that intelligence is passed down through the mother — surprise, ding-dongs! — and so men should make a point of marrying mentally up instead of down, in the case of Daddy, being older, and my mom, being younger and not so attuned upstairs. I mean, she never went to university, even, which is unusual in this neighbourhood. I follow her that way; it's not exactly as though I am imbecilic towards learning, it's just that I'm not all that interested in what they have to say in school, not enough to keep my short-sighted attention riveted. Put fairly, I am a shallow human being in regards to learning. I think I have other qualities but nobody else has discovered them yet. Like, I'm really good with animals and am sympathetic to poor people. I have a gift for reading newspapers. I'm not squeamish. I didn't mind my old horse, Gardenia, kicking it, or Walrus either, even though I had known them both for a very long time. They were old and it wasn't a tragedy; Daddy had been trying to get Mom to have Walrus put down and she wouldn't. Gardenia was glue-factory material, too creaky to brush the flies away. I kept her face in a fly guard and that made her feel better. Rita Lee started calling her Bandit. Rita Lee had a kind of outrageous attitude sometimes that was hysterical. "There's a bandit in our field," she'd whisper in her fake Southern accent, and make up a whole poem to go with it: "There's a bandit in our field, we better look out; bandit in our field, make us jump and shout." Irrational like that, nonsensically immature. However, it was fun before gin started oozing out her pores.

Millie and I were at a glass table on the periphery of the The Veranda, where waiters in striped waistcoats served us. The railroad track went along the beach in a mishap of planning (Daddy again), but the hotel had done its best to disguise the sound of occasional trains. They had tiers of colourful waterfalls — lights under phony clumps of lava rock — one level below us in the magnolia gardens where they kept hothouse gardenias and orchids. It was all ostentatiously sick but I personally didn't mind; I'm drawn to the hollow and trashy. The ocean that we could see clear enough was mute, overcome by the predictable splashing of circulating water.

Millie said Russ was feeling perfectly awful too, devastated. He'd been over to visit Mom the day before, to check in on her while Daddy was travelling. It was sort of an arrangement the grown-ups had, although I as a reader of Gothic novels wouldn't have allowed it if I were Millie or Daddy: who knew when a heart would go wayward? If Millie ever thought anything was going on, I guess she wouldn't have allowed those private visits, but I think they had all adjusted over the years, that Russ and Rita Lee were best friends. I mean, you'd come into the room and the two of them would be energized, laughing, arguing, but friendly, not like the arguments between Rita Lee and Daddy. She wouldn't drink as much, either, when Russ was there because Russ was a teetotaller, not because he had to be, like alcoholism, but because he didn't like the taste. He thought wine tasted too winey, for example. He was tall and skinny and an accountant, a boring occupation; but that didn't keep them from having a kazillion words running back and forth between them.

"He loved her you know, Rozzy," said Millie, ordering her third drink. "Not in the way you young people think. No, they were soulmates and had deep, unfathomable connections in another life." Millie believed that, even while she stumbled over the word "unfathomable." She did rebirthing and past-life regressions with people. Rita Lee, who was skeptical, said people would be zoomed back into another life and find out they were the queen of Egypt or they'd remember what it was like being born into this life and, really, how they were sorry they'd bothered. Millie tried saying "unfathomable" again but I told her it was too hot to bother with big words. I was thinking about Rita Lee and Russ. I don't know much about love; I'm still a virgin, which nobody would believe if they knew. You're expected to have made it at least a couple of times by age fifteen, and here I am way beyond, almost eighteen. If anybody asks, I belong to the New Christian teen movement and I'm saving myself for marriage. (A laugh.) I read about them in the paper.

Millie was feeling better after the third daiquiri. "I understand how your mother got into drinking," she said, putting down the glass. "It's so comfortable to just haze out."

You couldn't tell what her eyes behind her Ray-Bans were doing. "Your mother wasn't happy. She wasn't a happy woman."

I waited for her to continue but she fell silent, as adults do at the most profound points. I told Millie what I'd never told anybody, just to test it out: "When I disappear? They think, like, I'm at a friend's house — they just assume I am, Mom hardly ever bothered to call, check it out — but I was at that mission, the one on Fourth? They let me sleep on a cot they have in a room behind the kitchen. I go there and volunteer after school sometimes and Rita Lee figured I was hanging in the mall!" I laughed, almost choked on my Coke. I added, "She never asked me."

The rest I kept guarded, how I put the food — peanut butter and canned corn (everybody likes canned corn and hates green beans) and spaghetti, white bread from the freezer if we had bread, canned tomato sauce and Kraft macaroni and cheese dinners — into plastic grocery bags. Some East European people didn't know you're supposed to add milk and butter to the cooked macaroni and I found that out because a woman with a massive amount of steel in her teeth and really cracked lips turned down a box of this and I was trying to tell her how good it was, how her kids would groove on it, and she did this thing with her mouth like "sticky" and I got it, and then me and Fran, this lily-white Protestant who was there with me, we gave a cooking lesson, using the cat's water bowl for a pan and a box of powdered milk and so on. Pretty cool. This lady, like, flushed bright red from covering her mouth and laughing at herself so hard.

Millie was watching me. She lowered her shades to her nose and peered over them. The sun was on her left brow. "You are amazing, Roz," she said. "I had no idea. Your mother, either. We talked about you — of course, darling, we did, we worried about you. We lost touch the last little while. She wouldn't talk much to anyone. Except Russ, of course. But he doesn't talk to me!"

She said this last to be a joke but I understood adults and their "jokes." Acting is how they get past the hard places. That's why they can spot bad acting in movies and on TV. They say, like, Oh that's so unbelievable, did you see that expression? It's because they know; they perform all the time. I've been close enough to know all the compromises adults make. That's why I'm bulimic; I don't intend to be one, I intend to stop my body processes from maturing. That's what the shrink says I'm doing and I hadn't thought about it quite that way. I'm not an elite-level gymnast, my build is too big, but they suffer from the little-girl syndrome: they have to stay small and young and then Bela will love them and the American audience will too, especially if they perform while wounded and in pain. The shrink said those girls and I had the need for approval in common.

Millie was saying something about Aunt Nan and Uncle Larry.

I woke from my pseudo-Olympic dream. "What?"

She started over. "You can't live in this hotel forever, darling. You need someone to look after you, besides your super-busy dad. He's got another trip. You'd be happier with *family*, darling. I would take you instantly, you know I would. But I've got these weird commitments from here to Hawaii and on to Mexico. Arranging workshops. Although — I hadn't thought of this — you might come along." She stopped to assess me, maybe remembering the psychological mess that she was addressing.

Now I felt deluded, like Daddy'd deliberately sent her to talk to me; they were in collusion and I was being manipulated. He hadn't run it past me that he was going anywhere, so how did she know?

"Let's head in," Millie suggested. "I'm frying out here. I think I drank too much and talked too much." She rose, slipped her sandals back onto her feet, holding the table for balance. I insisted on writing the tab to Daddy's room. Millie was looking grey around the gills. "You wonder about how spiritual you are when you drink this much in an afternoon," she muttered mostly to herself. I have been thinking about spirituality, and as far as I know, Mom and Walrus and Gardenia simply disappeared into the ether.

We entered the chilled lobby, air conditioning at max. Sound of harpsichords, hushed voices; Turkish carpets. I looked at the greys and beiges and creams and taupes of the walls and got depressed. Rita Lee didn't believe in propriety. The parts of our house that she lived in were forest greens and mauves and sunflower yellows. I felt borderline faint. Millie reached for me, but I twisted away, uncaring about what the deadwood in the lobby trying not to look at me thought. I didn't give one damn iota, like Rita Lee used to say. A man handed me his handkerchief as I raced towards the elevators. The handkerchief was clean and had a monogram on it. You never knew who was in the world with you at any moment, that was my brainstorm. The elevator rose, I could hardly tolerate how long it was taking. I dashed down the hall, my hand put the card in backwards, the door didn't open, I was in a radical panic that I was on the wrong floor and she was inside our suite, unpacking her suitcase from a trip she forgot to tell me about. I accomplished the door, pushed it, lunged inside, darted through the place, checked out the bathrooms, the bedrooms, Daddy's office. She wasn't there. The rooms smelled of Lysol and air conditioning and new towels. I went back to my bathroom, stood at the sink, looked at it, barfed up french fries from lunch that came out in a froth of brown carbonation. God, I had to chew better. Clots everywhere and stuck in the drain. I cleaned up using tissues from the wall dispenser. The back of my throat burned. The whole scene was really gross. Really deadly gross. I was calmer.

I packed my overnight bag and took one last look around. I didn't leave a note for Daddy; his insincerity and betrayal were too ultimate.

"*Hola,*" Mr. Juarez said from the storeroom where he was unpacking a box of cold cereals. I revered Mr. Juarez, who came from Peru or Chile or Bolivia and had a gentle manner and kindly, wrinkled eyes that looked like he had seen it all and consequently had amassed a genial acceptance of everyone and everything. In the Spanish fashion, he greeted individuals enthusiastically and courteously, with no judgement behind his eyes. It was cool being around him, although he, like other people who worked at the mission, had a hassled quality, like his car was always breaking down, or he was helping someone else whose car had broken down and now he had to unpack the food shipment because there was no one else to do it who knew where to put things. We worked together slicing open the cartons and carting the various boxes, Trix and cornflakes mostly, to the shelves and he put some of the stuff, like canned white asparagus and canned crab that somebody thought would be a treat for poor people, on the shelf marked Camp because the mission also ran a Christian camp as part of their outreach. He put boxes of Red River hot cereal there, too, which the camp cook would know how to prepare. Down at the other end of the narrow room, Mrs. Thompson, a retired schoolteacher, was working at the computer, and she was always friendly even if her hearing wasn't so good, there was quite a lot of noise at that end, people speaking loudly so she could find their names on the computer and her asking, "Spell that," which of course was an amazing request considering the people right then were Vietnamese or Thai and didn't know our alphabet but I guess it was her teaching them, because she'd look at their welfare cards or their immigration papers and then start spelling the name and make them repeat after her. I was thinking judgementally, and Mr. Juarez saw my look and winked at me and I could tell that being in the midst of mayhem with all the babbling from around the world and the wall of shelves holding boring survival food and the Mexican ladies going through the clothes in the next room with their kids running in and out was what life was, I mean, like, this was it. Then when the phone rang and somebody from the office buzzed for Mr. Juarez, he walked by Mrs. Thompson's table and held his nose, shook his head, and I went down to that end of the room and, God, besides the usual mildew and old clothes, there was a corrupt smell that almost gagged me. I looked around, including under the table where Mrs. Thompson was sitting, and she went on with a Vietnamese woman who was stuttering in a language nobody understood and pointing to her stomach, which we could see was bloated, and then I spotted it, a bulging canvas sack that had got wet somehow. Rotten canvas was masking putrid, blackening potatoes, which was sort of like the smell sometimes in the root cellar where Walrus hung out, when he was an old dog but alive. Mom had insisted on a root cellar because, being Canadian, she liked to can things like chutneys and bizarre relishes that nobody would eat.

"Nice donation," I said, pointing at the sack, but nobody in line smiled, they just shrugged, including the Asian woman, and I thought maybe Mrs. Thompson's nose didn't work so well either, or else she was a first-things-first kind of person and feeding people was more important than smells. I was wondering how to clean it up

when the schizophrenic came through the side door — he
was lanky and long-haired and had an intensely comical
manner — and sniffed and said, "Yukoroonie, now this
is loony," and spotted the rotting sack right away and then
he went to the kitchen, I guess, because he came back with
a bucket of soapy water, a mop and a garbage bag and
worked around everyone and cleaned it up. I carted the
garbage out when the time came. Then he gave me his
card that read, "Detecting What Others Don't Know" —
that's all — and because it was just about four o'clock,
when the food distribution section closed, I worked my
way through the maze to Georgia Markham's office in the
other part of the building to tell her the story of the potatoes and to ask her if I could stay the night, because she was
the administrator for the mission who made major deci-
sions. We all liked the schizophrenic except when he was
overstimulated and talked messianically.

At four p.m., the mission had a close-of-the-day sort
of ritual like what Daddy and Rita Lee did with gin martinis when they were home together, and it was a minorly
pressured event, everybody signing off telephone conver-
sations or easing out the last of the foodies in order to
gather round a big old table and say prayers. Sometimes I
stayed and sometimes I didn't. Georgia was on the phone
when I stood at the door of her tiny office and she saw my
overnight bag and raised her eyebrows at me, but I wasn't
sure what she meant so I just moved along to the prayer
table and was the first one, for a change. I sat with folded
hands and concentrated on the cross, a very non-Catholic

plain one hung on the wall. The room, like the whole building, was a concrete bunker although the walls were painted a sky blue, with just one window that had a K-Mart sheer curtain almost long enough for it; on the floor were scuffed grass mats. The table had cigarette burns and other indignities etched into it but Georgia, who didn't pay attention to superficial appearances, usually brought cut flowers because her husband was a gardener, although there weren't any flowers today, just a brown-rimmed vase where water had evaporated out and next to it a pile of photocopied flyers advertising the camp. The room had cardboard boxes stashed here and there, filled with an unknown quantity, as Georgia put it, of non-food items, and there was a typewriter on the floor that was broken that someone was going to fix sometime. The room was also the library so there was a shelf with Christian-message books on it and a tattered upholstered chair with a pillow for your back and a doily on one of its arms. The room had a bare quality compared to the house I used to live in but it was excellent in its own way, chilled; there was a wall clock that went click occasionally although not anything you could predict, like it wasn't exactly clicking on minutes. I waited and listened to the clock. The building went suddenly quiet, suddenly too quiet, like I had gone deaf, and I knew something was wrong. Suddenly I went from depressed to abysmal. The sensation was ruthless: the vacancy where there had been fullness, silence where there had been sound, life and now there was no life, the sense of moving fast making me breathless with alarm, alarm,

alarm and then Georgia said, "That was your father on the phone," and I came crashing in and started shaking like an addict and Georgia took a step back like she was scared. This tripped me up more, but I could hear her phone ringing, but she didn't answer it, she pulled out a chair next to me and said like Rita Lee used to do when I was little, "There now, there now," and then I lurched into tears, a flagrant display, clutching the surface of the table like it could save me. "Jesus is with you," Georgia said. "He understands your suffering and grieving," and I didn't know that was what was happening to me until Georgia said it. I threw myself sideways into her surprised arms. She held her head stiffly away from my tumble of hair that Mom admired, Mom always envied my hair. Mrs. Thompson brought a roll of toilet paper for me to blow my nose on and Mr. Juarez patted my chair on his way past and a student from another office came in and tiptoed to the far end of the table. I asked, "Where's Eva?" because I wanted Eva there, she'd let me help her, and Mr. Juarez said, "She's not work here any more. She left, took another job," and I was zoomed out again because I cried, "She didn't say goodbye." Which of course she didn't need to, it's not like we really knew each other or anything serious. I slipped out to the kitchen and stood at the counter, using half a roll of the toilet paper during prayers that I could still hear, and when Georgia prayed for me, tears unloosed again, and then they prayed for Mike, who was from Bangladesh, who managed the food ordering and donations. He had a wife and a deviant for a son and a sickly daughter and a mother and one or all of these people were perpetually in some kind of trouble. His eyes were elusive or else he faced you squarely, but he was not present, he was always flying off, in body or mind, kind of like Daddy that way. Once I had to tell Mike we were running out of jars of baby food and he gaped at me like I was from Mars.

Georgia put a Swanson chicken dinner for me in the microwave before she went home. She had decided to let me spend the night on the cot off the kitchen, but she said I couldn't stay over any more because, really, they weren't a facility for runaways and also my father would call the police if I didn't go back to the hotel in the morning. Mr. Juarez said good-night and soon I was alone in the bunker, holding myself together with my arms, under the scratchy army blanket, the pillow smelling of cheese.

*

THE OTHER ROOM

FROM MY TERRACE — they call it a terrace here at the Frances Hill Retirement Residence, but it's just big enough for me and a coffee mug — I see the town of Ruth off in the distance, a staid hodgepodge of wood and stucco storefronts, narrow roads, elaborate old houses with bay windows and turrets mixed in beside the no-nonsense rectangles that pass for new dwellings these days. The Tide's Inn Hotel stands out because the bottom three storeys are painted a salmon colour, perhaps to fool tourists in this rainy climate into thinking that by some miracle they've landed in Mexico. The summers, I'm told, are unreliable here. The top storey of the Tide's Inn is a band of white stucco, broken by a criss-cross wood motif in the Bavarian style that runs rampant through so much of Ruth. Beyond is the lake, but it is the hotel that fascinates me. I never tire of wondering who stays there and why. A TV show could be designed around a small hotel, and each week viewers would witness "Life in Another Room." I think I could do well with this idea. For now, I just look at those small windows and wonder.

It's almost 10:10, which is recess time in the elementary school yard directly below my terrace. The school building has an old-fashioned look, ornate, with tall windows and double doors and cornices and spindles. With binoculars I can watch the children in the yard. Their noise rises up to me on my terrace at 10:10 every weekday and again from

12:30 to 1:30. At these times the children are let loose from the building and enter the outside in knots of bright fall clothing; they wear iridescent colours like exotic Amazon River birds. They cluster and yell together in the intoxicated, shrill voices that only children have. Children do not hear themselves; despite their striving for being grown up they don't realize that adults in a milling mass don't squeal and shout the way they themselves do.

Through my binoculars, I have taken to watching one child in particular. Twice a day, and occasionally at other times, I keep my eye out for him. I am learning about him, biding my time and simply observing him closely. I know more about him than his mother does. I know how he plays or doesn't play with the other children and that his timing is impeccable. When he withholds himself from the others, they follow him, whining. When he leads them in play, the whole yard gathers round, pushing and shoving to get close to him. Yet on other days he sits straight-legged on the bare ground, watching them as I watch him. He doesn't cover his face or hide himself when he wants to be alone. He is able to be alone in the midst of them. How they know not to bother him, I cannot surmise. It has something to do with the power he has over them at other times. They don't lose respect for him when he wants his privacy.

I almost said, It *had* something to do with his power.

As though his life had been lived in the past. Which it may have been, to a point. When I peer through the binoculars, I have sense enough to be wary of what I see and wonder if I am looking backwards in time, wonder if the school and the play yard exist or if they are merely an exit in my mind that I choose to take a couple of times a day. When I say I know this boy better than does the woman who thinks she is his mother — I've seen her, she works in the Overweightea grocery store, her name tag says June — I know this to be true even though I haven't bothered to find out the child's name. I don't need to.

Because he was mine, before.

Years ago, back then, for instance, long before I came to live in Ruth, when I was twenty-five and newly married, I awoke one twilight in a familiar bedroom, the one with the three-sided panorama of windows. I slid out from under the feather-weight satin quilt and searched for the blinking red light on Signal Hill, where they kept the oil wells in Long Beach, California. The purpose of the red light was to warn away planes when the fog was in, to protect, for instance, a plane flying in low from the ocean, its pilot not expecting a solitary hill so close to the sea, his eyes not paying attention to the navigation map on the seat beside him (which elucidates elevations in delicate linear spirals) but to the instruments. In foggy conditions the horizon is lost, sight and the inner ear disconnect and the pilot's brain tilts out of balance. He is intent on his turn-and-bank indicator, intent on keeping himself, embraced as he is within the capsule of the plane in fog, on the straight and level. Always the goal, they tell me, this straight-and-level business. That's what Karl says, anyway. Karl, who I am told is my husband, is a private pilot and knows about flying. He knows, I think, about surviving.

Through the wisps of gathering fog, I spied the red light that blinked soothingly, rhythmically machine-like, into the curtainless windows on the top floor of the old house. It was a fishbowl of a room, I realized, and the thought arriving so unexpectedly made me lift my arms and glide and whirl in the small space between the twin beds. I was having such a good time flying between the two islands, until I remembered who I was and where. I remembered that Karl had taken away the double bed after the baby was born.

I was flung into the open room, dizzy and trembling in its vastness, breathing hard, looking down at my real self: the belly flat and empty, the baby born.

They were trying to keep his being in the world from me. But I had proof: my belly was empty, skin still loose. Because I am blonde, my skin is not elastic, it's dry, thin stuff, that's what the doctor says, at least I think that's what he says, holding his warm palm on my cold tailbone as I sit, legs dangling, between the stirrups on the end of the examining table, while he bends over me and talks about my belly, my light, wispy pubic hairs curling out above the blue modesty cloth that lies lightly on my thighs.

I see myself as a character in a movie, and in my movie I shake myself clear of this probing, sweat-smelling doctor and put one bare foot in front of the other until I am down the stairs and in the kitchen. Karl Malenko likes his food; he's famous for it. His sister immediately pokes her elbow into my thin side and says, "Karl likes fat in his food." She winks. There is something lewd about Karl's sister, I don't know what she means by the wink. Madeleine is always hanging around, even though she has her own place and is supposed to have her own friends. I expect to find her in the kitchen, ensconced in the nook with something buttery in her mouth, when I fly around the corner in my bare feet, but Madeleine isn't there.

We never talk about the baby. They say I imagine things in the silence of the kitchen nook, as I try to remember how to set the table without looking at the note taped to it. I lay out everything from memory, like a preflight check-list, tick off the items: salt, fork, napkins, soup spoons, tea-spoons, plates. Now I will have to think what to put on the plates. I myself am not hungry, am becoming spindly. The doctor says I am pining away. Maybe that's what he says. He chews gum and is hard to understand.

While opening the heavy cabinet doors that Karl made, looking inside for something, a can to open would do it, I think of blasting my brains out with a shotgun or else tak-ing the butcher knife, the one Karl keeps sharp to cut his meat with, and plunging it into my throat, the hollow of my throat would be best because it's soft there and throbs. Instead, I change the place of the lightweight everyday fork beside Karl's empty plate to the right of the light-weight everyday knife, then move it back. My hand takes up shaking, tips the ceramic rooster pepper shaker, and pepper pops out of his back onto the red-checked vinyl.

Now the table is in on the tricks. The room becomes as

unreliable as those fun-house mirrors that I have stood
in front of and stuck my tongue out at, tongue the size of
a mouse tongue, and my belly button, the soft kind that
protrudes, looking obscene, a penis in the grotesque fat-
ness of my bare middle, and the legs sticking out of shorts
like pencils, maybe, or the legs of cranes. The table quakes
beneath my two palms. I wait for the clatter of cutlery, the
tinkle of dishes behind their massive doors, but there is no
sound other than myself breathing.

Madeleine enters the kitchen, her coarse, horse-
textured hair in a ponytail. In her arms she carries a bucket
of Kentucky Fried Chicken. "I thought you might be having trouble getting something together, so here." This is
kindness. "You miss the baby, don't you, Maryrose, dear?"
This is mean. Madeleine's eyes narrow into watchful
meanness so quickly that I stumble backward in time.

I was okay, really, right after the baby was born, and
recall an antique bassinet newly refinished in white lac-
quer that I painted myself, that lay near the fireplace
where Karl made bright flames leap. Watching the flames
made my mind begin its spin. I stare into Madeleine's
piggy eyes. I lost the baby in fire, I was shovelling my own
baby into a brick oven, roasting it.

Then the dream clicked in, with its clouds of provoca-
tiveness and obscurity, and became confused with the
image of the roasting baby, its tiny fingers curling into
blackened claws: not much flesh, not yet fed and fattened.
Something malevolent in the air, and I, as mother, take up
watchful dreaming.

Karl told me to smarten up. Dreams are not life. Madeleine told me to fatten up. "Your man, he doesn't like a cinder. I should know." I tried. I invited my friend Abby over for tea and cakes but could not make out what Abby was saying. Her kids, her cats? And was it Abby who patted my arm: "Maybe you're pregnant again, it would be the best thing — ?"

The baby's sudden death (that night I stole into his room and found him gone) seems to be the cause of what they're calling my breakdown; but "she always was a dreamer." Some aunt said this; it's the glib sort of thing an aunt who knows it all would say. Karl discovered me between semesters, struggling through Sartre and tanning at Tofino. I was tall and blonde enough and Karl, laughing and standing over me blotting out the sun, said, "I like my women with meat on them, but you will do," and then Madeleine came up behind him, put her pudgy, beringed fingers on his waist and giggled, "Oh yes, she will do, you silly man." Maybe that's what Madeleine said. I can't remember.

I wonder, Is there meaning in that meeting that I am missing? Am I the victim of a new conspiracy? Do they intend to use me as a *Lebensborn* breeder and steal my babies? It's not likely, altogether; and yet the world is not reliable, too much is uncertain. Oh, I was mentally wobbly before the baby's death, I was always perplexed by time past and time present. Who can say for sure where we are on that continuum? Or perhaps it's even worse. Perhaps we skip into a parallel universe, bring back fragments. The bedroom upstairs, for example, that I saw as so small. Once, hand in hand with Karl the first time we stood in the wide doorway, him smiling sweetly (recalling that smile makes the idea of conspiracy unthinkable, ridiculous), I said, "What a beautiful, spacious room!" And it was then, I wasn't mistaken. I said it, it was true and justifiable, before the trouble, before the baby died.

I was the happiest mother on the obstetrical floor, everyone said so. "I know it will be a boy, a son for Karl," I had smiled at the ceiling, scrupulously white, and closed my eyes and didn't need to see the baby at all. Something was wrong, however, they were too quiet, the nurses and the doctor. That she wouldn't look? That the baby was already a cinder? That she gave birth to air, foul air, her birthing one long fart? Is that what gagged them? No. It was fantasy, that moment. I heard the cry. And when my son was only three hours old, I was dancing through the hospital corridor, because it was dizzying, it was heady, this business of giving birth, and I was the happiest mother on the floor.

Home by the fire, dressed in my black dress, Karl having said, "I want you. Dress for me." The slight stretching of the stitches hurt but he was small, careful, I was tight, it was nice for him for once. My blood was wan and pinkish, not burnt red, and sponged easily off the carpet with cold water. I knew the baby was asleep there, somewhere nearby.

I stop the movie; I've seen it countless times. I undo myself from the projector of Madeleine's eyes and go to the sink, squeeze out a dishcloth, return full of purpose to the table and wipe up the spilled pepper. "Would you like to stay for dinner?" I ask, the perfect hostess, raising my head and showing my teeth the way I remember people do when they intend friendliness.

At the table there is fast eating, fast chewing, head-bent intentness of the brother and sister. The coleslaw mashes between their lips, the Colonel's juicy sauce leaks out the corners of their mouths. They scrape with knives the carton of mashed potatoes to ensure that none lingers in the circular crevices of the carton's bottom, and Karl sticks out his tongue to catch the drops of salty gravy from the Styrofoam tub he holds above his mouth. It is a joke, this Tom Jones style of eating. Karl and Madeleine laugh as they do it. They have said, as they say now, "It's our parents' fault, this disgraceful eating. But you should see our brother, Boris. Him, he's a wolf." They laugh. They like making Boris the worst one. All the meals of their growing up, their father talked of being hungry in Germany after the war. When the father thought no one was looking, he licked his plate. "Like a dog's," Karl told me when he still talked to me, "his tongue was long and flat." The father is dead now, and Karl and Madeleine eat to carry on the family tradition.

Maybe because my nap was shattered by the dream — or maybe because of the plump chicken thigh I bite into to be part of their merriment, that makes my teeth feel sick — I find I have to lower my face to hide the tears trickling alongside my nose. "How can you eat when the baby is dead?" I ask.

The reel spins and the film flaps, slapping the air like a whip. The sound, also, has gone out of the machine. Karl, wiping his mouth with the napkin I so carefully placed beside his plate, starts to relate a dream. In it, he is an SS *Obersturmführer* whose speciality is the incinerators where the babies go. He doesn't mind; their bodies are so small, they burn fast. Their crying, if they are awake, doesn't last long. Besides, it is innocent crying; they cry because they don't like the momentary sensation of weightlessness that occurs in the space and time after they leave the long-handled shovel, before they hit the ash pile. "You have to picture it," he says. Or maybe they don't like the momentary sensation of heat. "In any event, their crying," says Karl, "is irrelevant; they don't understand the long term, you know?"

Madeleine places her hands over mine that are splayed on the table. Madeleine's fingers are greasy; she isn't as careful as Karl. "Oh, poor girl," she blurts. "The baby isn't dead. He's with Auntie, remember? Just until you're better." Karl says, "She's forgotten again. Sweetheart? Sweetheart?" Poor *Liebchen*. This one has already lost her mind. She looked too long at the infant sleeping on the encrusted shovel. She looked too long before she sent her baby flying.

Red light blinking. My movie going again, I was in the bedroom with the twin beds. I was lying on one, the quilt pulled over my sad belly. Maybe I was lying on Karl's bed, maybe I was lying on my own, I didn't know. Maybe I was lying, all in all. Creating a reel for the fun of it. Or maybe I was chemically unbalanced, and it was that simple.

Surely, I thought then, a brain, grey lumpy cells congealed into a discrete anatomical formation, couldn't hold memories from one lifetime to the next.

Many years later I was in France, on the Normandy coast, looking out the window of the fifth-floor *pension* room that my baby brother found by ingratiating himself up and down the boardwalk, bargaining in his tattered bits of Parisian French to matrons who had pie dough on their roughened hands. I was cheered by the ocean, wild and green-blue, unlulled by the spring that was, despite the day's exciting, fierce weather, inevitably coming. The room had two beds, a sink and a bidet behind a curtain, a full bath across the hall. I had sat on everything, including the bidet, marking the room as mine.

Below, on the concrete boardwalk, forlorn umbrellas belonging to outdoor cafés were folded on their stalks, tails flapping in the gale. I was breathing hard, puffed out from climbing down the stairs to the shore, where the *pensions* were, and then up the winding staircase to our room, Gil carrying the luggage, I hauling only myself and my lumpy, institutional body, the other lithe and lovely one subsumed in the space of a dozen or more terrible years, although the years hadn't managed to eat up my height. I say the years were terrible because they have left me without a reliable memory in my head. Hospitals, halfway houses, clinics, the whole ball of wax: these types of life experiences are takers, they suck until you are purged of your nightmares and left parched in sterile corridors. When they are finished (when you are finished!), out you go, pounds and pounds heavier, crammed with starchy foods, foods fried with lard — so economical when you're cooking for a crowd.

Now I was on holiday, so they assured me, the people who gingerly took me back into the family, including this round, curly-haired boy of twenty-two — Gil, half-brother to me, born and raised in Montreal, who was out searching for a lemon for our gin and tonics. He was the only child of my father and his second wife, an unhappy Québécoise who thought she was through raising brats. They, the family, were all living in Paris for a few years, something to do with my father's work, some electronics business he is in. My father in my memory is hazy, and seeing him in person after so many neglectful years, he again struck me as evasive, the sort of man who chose to remain out of focus.

The ocean was calming in a way that Paris was not. I have always loved the roiling sea and the bracing air that goes with it. I opened the shutters, pressed my head into the wind, inhaled. The bay was large, embraced by long-armed cliffs. I hated Paris, the only person on the planet to entertain such a thought, so everyone would have had me believe. "How could you?" they cried, fluttering their hands. "This is the most beautiful city in the world, the most cosmopolitan, the most...," and they prattled on, as though I could care. I knew myself as I did not use to. I did not like Paris and said so.

The city was frightening, not for the obvious reasons — the traffic, the taxis, the haughty women who think themselves the centre of the universe, the expensive cafés, the incomprehensible telephones, the endless *croque-*whatevers which were all I knew how to order on my own. No, none of that was so awful. What I did not like was the swastikas hidden everywhere, on the sides of old buildings in alleys in the neighbourhood of Rambuteau that I found myself exploring. The swastikas were faded, half-heartedly scratched out or whitewashed, but they were on bridges crossing the Seine, on doors leading to cellars; there was a tiny one carved into the ornate wood of a toilet stall at a posh hotel my father took us to. To distract me from wandering into old neighbourhoods, Gil trundled me to Père-Lachaise to Jim Morrison's grave, and it may have been there, although I cannot be sure, that I became aware that the splicing tape holding me together was curling at the edges. What I mean is, I started acting as haunted as I felt. I took to scurrying, a form of movement ridiculous in a woman my height and not yet forty.

I was haunted in Paris not by the present — *that* all my doctors assured me I was prepared to handle — but by the upwelling past, elusive and not even mine. The war, for which I wasn't born, had taken on an embarrassing significance. I wanted to know everything about everyone I met. Where were you? What were you doing? I asked my father's colleagues, many of whom were old enough to have been adults there, back then, when Paris was captive, overrun with Germans. They had to have been doing something, those people who now wore expensive business suits and ties, their faces fleshy, their fingers comfortable around goblets of fine wine. I mean, what were you doing during the war? Did you fight? Hide? And when they took your neighbours away — well, here you can see why my father thought a holiday by the sea, with Gil as my guide, would be just the thing.

And off we went, Gil and I, by train and trolley, carrying our baguettes of fresh bread in his new embroidered bag. We were going along nicely when two conductors, young men in uniforms, halted beside our seats and demanded something in a tone that threw me into a fugue state; the dark-haired one reminded me of my ex-husband, Karl, a frightening man, unpredictable, menacing. And though Gil asked me nicely for my ticket, I could not unclench my hand to let it go. He apologized, said that I didn't speak French, which seemed all that was required to explain my behaviour. They spoke at length to Gil in the way the French do, and during my absorption, eyes closed and concentrating on removing Karl's coolly mean eyes from my mind, Gil slipped the ticket out of my grasp. We were on the wrong train, heading northeast instead of northwest. We were dropped in the middle of nowhere, at a deserted station hung with pretty baskets of fuchsia. After a while baking in the sun and wondering where we were, a small, one-car train pulled up and we sat at what I thought was the rear, on a curved platform seat with windows against our backs.

The car was full of women in kerchiefs carrying baskets of bread or little dogs, and there were girls with bare feet stuffed into pointy-toed black flats. When the train moved, it went backwards, from my point of view, and we were rushing head-first through the countryside, as though from a front-row seat in a roller coaster. Once, we descended partway underground into the semi-dark, wooden braces forming walls of dirt on either side of the track, and then, like a miracle, the ground we raced upon rose rapidly and we emerged into sunlight, as though in flight, to see a small boy waving a cap in a field. There was something familiar about him, even at that speed of travel; I knew him, I wanted to wave back, *Hello, hello*, but when I blinked, he vanished.

The trolley-train took us to the coastal town of Fécamp and there Gil and I, tired perhaps, had our first tiff. How to find the town, up the hill or towards the sea? Gil insisted we climb the hill and of course he was right, there was the village in the midst of a garden market, donkeys braying and children running in the drizzle over the slithery cobblestones. I headed directly to a store to hunt for Marie Brizard (I trusted her Quaker-like face) and Gil accompanied me and we argued briefly over what to buy. "I loathe cassis, I loathe anisette," Gil said. "Please, Maryrose, have pity, this is *France*." Neither of us wanted to add weight to our luggage by bottles of wine and I did not want anything so crass as whisky and so we did the English thing and bought gin and some tonic, too, and then climbed onto the bus and sat in seats across the aisle from each other, silent and petulant as quarrelling children, each staring out our respective windows.

The mood didn't last; after all, Gil was practically my own little one during the year his mother wasn't interested. His hair had my father's stiff curl, and Gil wore it longish in the style of artistic young people. Away from his parents he wore his earring and tended to stroke it as he talked. He had a beautiful singing voice. Our father thought it sissy for a boy to love light opera, which reveals the kind of man our father is.

The station in Étretat was deserted, an emptiness that made me nervous. I wanted to cry out, Where is everybody? — the cry from a favourite children's book I had read over and over to Gil while he cuddled, sucking his thumb, on my lap. A small white car raced past us, shrilling. I moved so that my shoulder touched his. "You've brought a queen's load of luggage," Gil muttered, lisping. We began our hike towards the sea. I followed, suddenly light-hearted.

I was becoming aware of a terrible noise in my head when the door swung open and Gil burst in, his face agleam with news. "You won't believe it, Maryrose. You see the cliff, the one on the left?" He danced towards the window. "There are *tunnels* in those cliffs, from the war, if you can believe it. Like real, honest-to-God tunnels with cannons in them? And there are these tourists, a honeymoon couple, or maybe not, the story changed depending on who was telling it. Anyway, his leg is broken and they were trapped when the tide came in. He was probably performing some macho number for his yum-yum bride and went and damaged himself. I hear men do that sort of thing." He paused and giggled. "Anyway, m'dear, that's what the helicopter is about." And he pointed again, in the other direction, where yes, I finally noticed a helicopter dipping like a drunken bird against the gusts of wind, its propeller noise muffled in the general hubbub of sea and wind and the overdrive in my brain. This place was turning out to be unpredictably disconcerting, despite Gil's triumphant bringing forth of a lemon. He sat on the hope chest at the foot of the bigger bed and hacked at the lemon with the dull blade of his Swiss army knife. He splashed yellow wads into our waiting glasses.

"And I thought Étretat was going to be boring!" he chortled, by way of a toast. I, meanwhile, found myself staring at a wall where a movie was ongoing. Horses let loose from a stable, an old man weeping into his hands, a blur and a woman waving to a child on a bridge, a child waving a lace hanky, moving away with a smile on his face — and why not? Such a manly little one in wool knickers and cap and new big-boy boots, waving a hanky sewn by his grandmother, I knew that the old woman had sneaked it to him although I'd told her not to, they would think he was girlish, they would take advantage of him in obscene ways — and there he was, my baby with the soldiers, marching with the other children to a safe place, supposedly away from — oh, it was intolerable, the heat suddenly in the room, the flat tonic — like acid in my throat, the slick feel of my lemony teeth.

"Are you all right?"

I shook my head and sank onto the bed, handing my glass to Gil, and lay back, head swimming with voices arguing in a language I did not know. I lay still and listened intently. It was as if, if I tried hard enough, I would comprehend. "Did you ever have a lace handkerchief?" I asked Gil. I didn't mean to disconcert him, I wondered if I was flashing on an event that had happened between us when he was little. "Maryrose," he said. The warning in his tone made me sit up. Gil was old for his years, and he was used to me, but his eyes were desperately wide. The expression was familiar; when you're being crazy, people try so hard to encompass your words into their world that the effort makes *them* look unhinged.

"Oh, no. Goodness no," I said reassuringly. "I was just …thinking. If your grandmother on your mother's side was a doily maker. You know. An old lady who crochets everything in sight."

"You forgot, she died before I was born." His look was wary, but he poured me another gin. Handing it over, he took a breath. "Never knew her. Never knew anybody, except you. Mère took off for Montreal to stay with her girlfriend, Father was God-knows-where on business most of the time, even you went away. Jesus," he said and lifted his glass. "Hello, Geraldo."

In the morning I stood sideways to the mirror above the sink, checking if my pregnancy was showing. I could feel the wiggle of the worm of life in my uterus and for a moment I was ecstatic. What I saw in the mirror was just my usual saggy profile, the stomach of a careless eater. I touched myself, let the sadness move up to my awakening brain. Of course I was not pregnant, although I *knew* what it felt like, I knew everything about it, I knew about birth and that leg-wide, elemental giving forth. I pulled back the curtain and stepped into the room. Pregnant, indeed! Dreams were potent entities, creatures that found the vulnerable and played themselves out. In this one, I was my age, an older woman gratified by her first pregnancy. I had waited a long time for the event.

Gil came back from his walk and we breakfasted downstairs at our table, the concierge unfriendly to us, which Gil said was normal; she thought she'd been jewed down in her price. I commented that "jewed down" was a terrible expression.

"Well, I *do* know what you mean, but I didn't do it, jew her down, *she* just thinks so, it doesn't matter," he said flippantly, picking up his warm *café au lait* with both hands. He cocked an eyebrow. "And, newsflash, dearheart, someone's invited me to hear his Gilbert and Sullivan records. A nice boy. From Paris. I'll be out for a while." The croissant he bit into broke onto his plate and he collected the flakes by licking his fingers.

I had learned that when confusion arose, it was sensible to imitate another's actions, so I broke my own croissant, crunched into it. One doctor advised that I surround myself with people who were not entirely sure of their sanity; they would behave most naturally. People totally sure were most likely dangerous and should be avoided. He laughed, of course, as did I.

My omelette arrived dry but Gil, who usually noticed and corrected these oversights, was gaily going on: "I do feel Jewish, as a matter of fact, especially in Montreal. All my friends are Jewish, they're simply the most interesting people."

"You'll never make up for my lost son," I said.

We fell silent, except for chewing sounds that my ears picked out beneath every other sound, sounds that made me feel sick to my stomach. Saliva I don't like and never have, and my teeth and I have had a long and traumatic history: I scratch at them with my fingers, dig at them with my tongue, brush them excessively, and on one particularly unhappy occasion I was found trying to pull one out with tweezers. Except for bloody gums and a cut lip, the tooth survived. I don't know why I dislike them so much. Some behaviours you get to the root of, so to speak, in therapy, and some are mysteries of the brain stem, ancient, ancestral, genetically coded.

Gil suddenly intruded on my introspection. He placed his cup down. He said, "I'm not to blame for that. You know I was too young to be involved." He stood. His cheeks wore pink dots, like dabs of rouge. From his manner, I realized I'd done something harsh and inappropriate. I couldn't understand what he was talking about. My brain froze, unable to recall what it was. Gil bowed in my direction, left the dining room. Through the lacy curtains I saw him on the boardwalk, undecided about which way to go. I was left trembling with loneliness even while I performed show-the-teeth to everyone present, and then I shrugged, a shrug I hoped would come off as ladylike, nonchalant, genteel. Meanwhile my heart was dropping inside the shell of me.

The tide was out, past the end of the cliff that rose ominously high once I was picking my way across wet rocks and tide pools in the shadow of it. I could see an iron stair situated against the face of the cliff, quite far out, somehow attached. Earlier, from the room, I'd noticed people using the stair at low tide to get to the top of the cliff itself, where Gil had mentioned there was a walking trail. Within me tension was building because I did not know how long the tide had been out or when it would turn or whether, when it did, it would pounce. The distance between the docile, lapping waves that were ahead as I proceeded outward, and the seawall at my back, where the *pensions* and cafés were looking exceedingly small and remote, seemed enormous, perhaps half a mile; and I was a mere speck in this vast bay. If the sea were to change its mind about where it wanted to be, and were to grow determined to reach its high tide mark, it seemed to me the force necessary to go the distance would involve huge quantities of water accelerating shoreward, sweeping over anything in its way. I saw myself knocked off my feet, struggling in the froth, flailing, gulping, waterlogged by heavy clothes. And when I looked around, analysing my precarious situation, indeed there was no one else out so far as I was. A few people were lined along the shore and I wondered, as I tend to, if they knew more than I did. Did they know the tide was turning? And, pausing to squint over my shoulder, I wondered if someone was waving. And if that gesture I thought I saw was, indeed, a wave, was it a greeting or a warning? I almost stopped moving entirely but urged myself to puddle-jump faster, in order to make the rock face and the cliff top — I would have a story of bravery to relate to Gil. Finally I grasped the rusty stair and hoisted myself upon it. By the time I reached the top, I was in an internal commotion and wanted only to be down again and safely back in the room.

However, inertia had propelled me that far, and I followed the trail upward and saw, not far along, a small crowd gathered around a policeman in a yellow slicker. He was shouting into a bullhorn while the helicopter hovered importantly, a rope dangling from it. I supposed they were going to remove the injured man from the tunnel. I couldn't understand what the rope was for or what the people around me were saying. I thought perhaps something more complicated was going on. It was possible that she, the woman, was being held hostage by her new husband. I knew, somewhere in my mind, that such things had happened. Or that he had killed her because she had misplaced their child. The noise in my head was terrible again. The sky itself was overcome, sad and grey and drizzly.

Then I was scurrying, clambering down the stair, hurrying awkwardly across the endless obstacle of black rocks, the ocean breathing down my neck. I was afraid to look back. I arrived in the room, panting and frantic with a familiar claustrophobia. There was a note from Gil: "Mary-rose, back soon, please wait here." I began to whimper. I had missed him; now he was gone, and I might never see him again.

I found myself at the bus station, apparently having decided to take things in hand, to become a tourist and use this experience for personal growth, the phrase I had memorized from books and sessions with shrinks. I had scribbled a note for Gil, "I'm sorry. I'm all right," and moving fast, was loose in a loosened world.

I climbed onto the first bus, which was going to Yport up the coast, and took a seat behind an old woman — was the countryside filled only with old women? She was chattering to the driver, who let her out beside a little path that led into a new field; that done, the bus hurtled its too big, too modern self between the hedges marking the road. I disembarked into rain, beside a kiosk, without an umbrella or the map, which in my excitement to be on the move again, I had forgotten to bring.

The village was shrouded in dreary clouds coasting in low off the sea. I started to walk, raindrops assaulting me. All around a dead feeling made my bones uneasy, an ugly bottom-of-the-boat sort of smell, although it wasn't a particular odour that caused the assessment; rather, it was an instinct that rose behind my nose and made me wrinkle it. I hurried seaward, hoping for the thrill of breakers, my cape pulled as high over my head as I could get it and still peer out. The narrow streets were closed in upon themselves, the tight houses shuttered. I passed into the village centre and noticed a *boulangerie* and a few other shops, all mysteriously closed. I came to a confectionery that was open, and because the omelette was hours ago and I had forgone lunch, bereft over the loss of Gil, I was hungry.

I stepped into sweet fragrances, onto squares of black and white vinyl tiles. From an open door at the back of the store, behind the counters, I heard a radio. In a high trilling voice of women greeting each other, I called, "*Bonjour, madame*," and a young woman, a girl really, emerged apologetically, tying the sash of her crisp white apron. She curtsied, asked if she could be of assistance; that much I understood. And then, as happened to me when people were kind, or because I was drowning like a dog and grateful to be in the warmth of her shop, or because I was hungry and refused to give myself the gift of food — an old pattern based on pre-verbal guilt, something to that effect, my mind was not entirely clear — I stood tongue-tied and helpless. I was a statue puddling her clean floor.

A car in a hurry drew up to break the awkwardness of our situation. I glanced out the window eagerly. The vehicle, a black Mercedes, was as amazing a sight to me on these cobbled streets as my appearance and behaviour must have been to the curious and attentive girl. Car doors slammed and into the shop stomped three people, the two large women speaking German, ignoring me utterly, and busily pointing here and there and debating the merits of the cakes and petits fours and demanding that the girl take this out so they could inspect it, take that out, *Nein, oui, ja, ja,* that one, and shook their heads as they surveyed the lot, *Nein, nein,* not good enough.

Meanwhile, the man, round and short, his tight well-fed cheeks ruddy with a prosperous patina, sized me up. He was frank about it. As his deliberate gaze moved over my body, stopping at crotch and breasts, I remembered my long-ago life, how I used to feel bullied by Karl's eyes too, how I was crazy back then, but doctors don't like that word, they say "confused"; or if they are not quite so kind, they say "disturbed" in a way that implies mentally. A fog moved over the black and white tiles, my feet became lost in it. I looked up and the man, catching my eye, dismissed me with a twitch of the corner of his mouth. He turned to the women, who had chosen a few small cakes. The girl had put them in boxes, was finishing the boxes with red ribbons. Her face was dark.

When the sound of the car receded and the silence came again, I gathered my nerve and stepped forward. "*C'est dommage,*" I murmured.

She opened the case and handed me a chocolate truffle. "They are shitheads, all of them," she said.

When I returned to Étretat, Gil was at the *pension* next door to ours, sipping Cinzano, shivering in a short-sleeved plaid shirt and full of distraught drama when he saw me: "Oh, Maryrose, dear, I was in such a state," and so on, his eyes that lovely amber of his mother, Claire, whom I'd admired, mistakenly, when I was a girl. He feared he had lost me. What did he think had happened to me? I asked him. Did he think the whitecoats had come and taken away his old sister?

His blush notified me he did. Still, I was forgiving, having myself believed the bastards to be hot on my trail most of the day.

"Oh, you are soaked, you poor thing," he went on, and led me up the stairs and insisted I get in a warm bath, which he drew for me, and he laid out a fresh set of clothing on the bed and was sitting, his back to the room, reading by the one lamp, when I entered from across the hall, wrapped in a towel, and I remembered why I loved him as I dried and dressed and I remembered how much I missed him and the memories made me leak tears. "Now, now," he said, moving to comfort me, Gil the sudden mother, pressing his cheek to my shoulder. "I'm always here."

Which of course wasn't true. I was already seventeen when he was born, and enamoured of his glamorous mother, how straight her back was, how lovely her clothes, the thick diamonds on her fingers given her by her husbands. That she already had three children in their twenties didn't concern me; the new baby and I were the ones at home in that big house, us and the full-time maid, who neglected the baby although he was part of her job. I didn't mind that, either, her neglect; while I rushed home eagerly from high school to hold the skinny little fellow, he for his part gurgled with joy at the sight of me; and I used to pad my tummy with his baby blanket, imagining myself his mother. Though I was foolish and unwanted in that house, as he was, I imitated Claire at important moments. "*Non, absolument non*," she would say to the little Guillaume when he could toddle and wanted to touch her party dress. And when one night it thundered and he crawled into my bed, I turned him out, saying in her haughty tone, but in English, "No, you are a big boy now. Leave me alone, I need my beauty sleep." And he lay on the floor, clutching the bedskirt. I knew, because when I awoke near dawn, there he was. I almost stepped on his head, stumbling to the can. He was two.

Gil brought us up a cold supper and a bottle of *vin du pays*. It began to rain.

In the night I awoke to the sound of a shutter banging. The sound was muffled so that I quickly realized it wasn't our shutter, and then when I could not seem to wake up, I noticed there were goings-on in our room, that we were inhabited by strangers who didn't notice us. Because of the warmth and ease of the evening and the comforting sound of the steady rain, I felt safer than usual. I rose out of my body to the ceiling, breathing as softly as I could because I was fascinated by events that unfolded without my prompting. The movie was on, I thought, that's all. Here now, a plump mother was dressing a sweet little girl, dark ringlets down her back — how patient one must be to get them even-sized as these ringlets were, I knew without ever having attempted a curl in my life. The child was about three years old, the age Gil was when I finally left him at my father's house to go to school.

But she was speaking, this other woman, to the child,

who was flipping her head, playing with her hair, exposing the tender wisps of dark down on her nape. The mother persisted. If you hear the soldiers knocking on the door, go to the hope chest and take out the pretty little pinafore and put it on. In the pocket is a hanky that Grandmère made for you. In the hanky is gold jewellery. Go to the bakery and wait for a nice yellow-haired lady and walk up to her and curtsy like the sweet dumpling you are and put your hand in hers and say you can pay. Tell her you have lost your mother.

The woman didn't speak the story all at once; she was, after all, talking to a child. The child was impatient, *Oui, Maman, oui, oui, je le sais, je le sais,* she interjected, stamping her little foot — she was spoiled, I thought it obvious — but the mother made her repeat the instructions until, really, I found myself slightly exasperated too. Anybody could tell that the child was clever. When the mother was satisfied, she lifted the little one into bed, tucked her in, caressed the shiny cheeks. You almost forgot, the child said, petulant. I am to practise this, and then her hands made the sign of the cross. You are my heart, the mother replied.

Then Gil groaned in his sleep and startled us all. I found myself back in my cold bed, heart pounding. Waves were splashing onto the beach pebbles, pulling them out, rolling them back. The wind had come up. The shutter banged, and this time it was ours. I crossed the bare floor, touched Gil's hairline where bubbles of perspiration had gathered. "Would you like to get in with me?" I whispered.

My fingers smoothed his forehead, the slickness evaporated under my warm palms. My heart felt bruised, as though, as a result of some dreadful omission, I had caused it irrevocable damage.

Gil smiled, the familiar gas-bubble smile of an infant. "No," he sighed, either in answer to my question or to an inner narrative that excluded me. He turned towards the wall and I drifted back to bed. I watched him sleep; I wanted to apologize for having the gall, for one remote second, to assume that there would always be a living child, a child who had survived. I wanted to be his guardian angel. I heard my voice, "*Je voudrais...*," and there rose in me an ache I couldn't name. A rush of moist cold to the nipple: milk leaking from my left breast. Impossible. A dizzying, embarrassing dampness. I touched myself furtively and was reassured it was nothing. An illusion, caused by rain, a gutter splash, memory.

———

Boris Malenko, my ex-brother-in-law if he's anything to me, found me in the Clarke Institute of Psychiatry in Toronto and brought me west to Ruth. They said I was in trouble again and, in this instance, I agreed. I could *feel* the trouble on my skin, with the dead spirit cells that were resting upon me like layers of mite dust.

In Toronto I went to a doctor, a homeopath, who could get away with charging me an arm and a leg for his services because he sensed my desperation. I sensed his sensing. I had become so worrisome to myself that I didn't waver about paying his outrageous fees. Like giving a talisman to a witch doctor was my handing over that wad of money. If I was charged enough, I believed the dead spirit cells would leave me. I was knee-deep in the new theory, about decayed spirit matter. It was invisible and everywhere, floating in the air. A person going through an uprooting or a life transition was more susceptible to attracting invisible decayed spirit matter, which acted as a plug, enhancing claustrophobia and the feeling of being trapped. The feeling was real, because the person *was* trapped: enclosed in an invisible film by used-up spirit matter, which was, by its very nature, lifeless.

Sitting across from the homeopath, I was thinking that if I could vacuum all my surfaces and simultaneously soak myself in wax, the dead spirit dust couldn't penetrate and I would be cured. I asked him, "Is my theory any crazier than colour therapy, magnetic realignment or sound waves?" (For I knew he believed in those treatments.) A bundle could be charged for the wax, money could be made. The wax would have to be special, allowing the skin to breathe in only new spirit.

The doctor gave me tincture of skullcap and St. John's wort to help me sleep.

It was obvious to me, as I left his office, that the doctor believed in himself. When I entered the subway, people rushing about down there seemed to as well, except for those of us covered with dead spirit matter, whose life force was dulled. I could spot us: we were the ones looking out of muddy eyes, our glances befuddled and at the same time challenging, never certain why we were on the subway or bothering to go home, if we had a home, and eat dinner, or even what the purpose of dinner was — a person could get that far gone. In my opinion, however, we were caught up in food; our eyes glinted greedily at the sight of it. Even the anorexics among us focused on food. They carried a terrible guilt from the other life, from stuffing themselves while others starved. Now they starved themselves — ghosts' revenge — so that they shrank to become the skeletons they saw in the camps while they themselves were hunched over steaming bowls, filling their faces with pork loins and sauerkraut, packing it in hand over fist.

There was more to it, I had it all worked out. It was a fruitless theory because the healing wax, so far as I knew, didn't exist.

Mornings in Toronto used to begin earlier and with a cigarette besides the coffee, but I have given up cigarettes — the Frances Hill is smoke-free, a torture chamber — and consequently am in a state of pain all through my body. Although it has been two months since I quit I am still asphyxiated from the cigarettes and feel that a lung has collapsed from the shock, perhaps dismay. The surprise of inhaling and exhaling empty air has sent my lungs — maybe one, maybe both — into a state of seizure, much like catatonia. The health industry would like me to believe that my lungs are rejoicing. But I know better. They hate their new condition, they hate it like hell itself.

In their protesting, they are reminding me of dying. The panic that the dying experience, which is a frantic gasping. Watch a goldfish out of its bowl. Picture a husband on his deathbed. Or imagine a son, and think how he will react, hoisting himself of his own volition into the gassing van because he is a good boy, because his mother has taught him well, she has — I have — taught him to be a good, obedient boy. At the end, he will gasp too. The mallet in this case is invisible. But it is there nonetheless.

Sometimes, before the ritual of the coffee-making, I turn on the shower and strip off my perspiration-soaked sleep clothes and step in. I like the water pounding on my head, the solid water pressure. As I turn and the spray attacks my face, I breathe deeply, sucking up a few droplets of water into my nostrils, letting them trickle down my throat, imagine myself drowning just as I begin coughing. However you lose your access to air — by fire, flood or gassing — the closing-down process is the same: the body's incredulity, its startled stillness and focused alertness concerning its imminent demise, its disbelief because it has struggled through so much, warded off insanity and chicken pox, survived the bicycle accident, the array of prescribed psychotropic drugs. It has done everything in order to live its cycle, to preserve within it the spirit of you, and now *this*, the unavoidable trap, the ultimate insult. The body panics and you panic with it. You will use your elbows to push old women aside, you will claw your way to the top of the pile to get the last suck of air.

I lie down in the tub, knees bent, the power of the

water like glossy beads pricking my plump abdomen, my fat middle-aged hips. Somewhere along the way, I gave up my girlishness. I rest the back of my head over the drain and the tub begins to fill.

Even with my various rituals, including the morning coffee-making, my mind, while improved since leaving Toronto, nevertheless slants towards a certain mental light-headedness. Before Boris moved me into the Frances Hill, which he and his wife run among their many endeavours in this little burg, I know I was again in the psych ward. It is the kind of thing that happens when you momentarily lose your place in the world, your sense of place, and act raving in the street. They capture you, confine you. But the rigmarole is silly, their concern unreal, and even more ridiculous, they treated me like a run-of-the-mill psychotic. I wasn't "acting out" at all, just upset one day, angry with myself for misplacing things. I had been dreaming again of a familiar child, the plump sturdy little one, playing with wooden alphabet blocks. He was wearing dark blue short pants and ran, stricken with fear over a minor misdeed, up the stairs to my left as I turned to face the door the police were banging on (in our naivety that was all the uniformed men were, simple police), and I glanced down from what seemed a long distance, saw my small feet clad in smart black shoes on the tapestried carpet with the fringe round the edge. I was caught in the rectangle of that rug, my life ensnared in the times, my future vanishing. There were probably over a hundred gathered on our street in Berlin watching us being taken away (my husband was a doctor who merited special treatment). We rode in the van, just our small family. I was angry at my husband; his complacency in believing in the basic decency of the human race had got us in this fix. I was so riveted on my anger that I neglected to comfort the frightened child. He was musical; I think of him with a violin.

I believe my son is in the world; I'm convinced he is out there. But that knowing, coupled with the rapidly evolving theory of dead spirit matter and the St. John's wort that didn't work, overwhelmed me. I was inappropriate in expressing emotion and Queen Street Mental Health nabbed me, transferred me to the Clarke. I know that the weary rage that attacks me from the other world can be contained. I just have to keep on guard more.

My difficulties may be partly due to the drugs I am prescribed, but mostly they are caused because I have an amazing ability to travel in my mind. Last night I was with my real husband — not Karl, who passed through my early life like a foul wind — in Vienna, I think, in a restaurant with another couple. The other couple looked like brother and sister to me, dark hair, dark eyes slightly protruding, willing smiles. He was wearing a burgundy beret; she a burgundy winter scarf. We were laughing, eating. I didn't know why we were behaving so merrily; she'd just had an abortion. She was so far along she'd had to take the train to Paris. She was so far along that in another two weeks she would have had a tiny handful of infant that parents nowadays invest so many prayers in. I don't know why I was there, laughing, eating, condoning.

Some women have body-blindness; I think the woman in the dream was one. When they are fat, they think they're thin; when big, small. When pregnant, body-blind women think they're sick because of something they ate. They so believe it that even their lovers (some of them married and fathers, who should know better) don't notice the round knot beneath their soft bellies. Some women are so body-blind, it isn't until labour they discover their pregnancy.

That was not the case with me. I was the happiest mother on the ward.

That recurrent thought woke me with a start. It took me a moment to recognize my small, plain bedroom here at the Frances Hill, to recognize the ridiculous, pink ruffled bedspread I lay under like a humoured, ageing child. Where that thought arises from escapes me. I fell back into a half-sleep. I saw my husband walking in an alley, poking along with a stick through rubbish, looking for something, but in a peaceful, unhurried manner. He was wearing a cap much like the one our little son wore in imitation of him, a flat-topped motorcyclist corduroy cap with a bill on it. (I call it a motorcyclist's cap, a term from the days of the first motorbikes. I do know that motorcyclists today wear helmets.) My husband was behaving very independently, neither pleased nor displeased to see me. With me were others, I am not sure who; but with me are always unnamed others. I am their tool, their means of expression.

Not in a horror-movie way do I mention the others who go with me; we all have them. What I mean are the various and sundry people who live inside me. They might be me, myself, in an old guise, from this life or others; they might be ancestors from my genetic past, or my half-brother, Guillaume, who perished of AIDS; or they might be strangers. During the rough period that led to my being in Ruth, the period after Gil died, many strangers on the subway were pressing themselves on me, in their need to make contact. Their desperation mirrored something in me, I plucked bits of them and carried those bits away. In this manner, others disseminate their characters, their traits, their personality and moods, through my motility. I am like a bird who inadvertently snags a dandelion seed on its foot and transports it to a new place. They, the doctors, explained away the theory of dead spirit-cell matter, but I am not entirely convinced there isn't something else going on. The theory is in the process of transformation.

But my husband in the alley was content to be alone in the nowhere place. I was just there, and saw him. He may have waved — there is always someone waving in my dreams — but it meant nothing. The wave, if he did wave, didn't budge him from his spot or stop his methodical searching. I think his mind was lost in the grieving for our son. He is so unlike Karl, who didn't care. Vaguely I recognized the parameters of the place where my husband poked about, as though I have seen it from the air. Finally, fully awake, I took out my map of Berlin and tried to locate him but wasn't able to. I want to describe where he was, in what part of the city. But there are no words; for all the strange things there are no words. The place may be merely a tremble in some backwards sphere of my mind. A vestigial place, near the brain stem, where collective memory is housed.

After such a busy night, I am cranky and grouchy. I want my nose in a coffee cup, even though the taste of coffee doesn't appeal. It's the ritual that continues, morning after morning. After a nice soak in the tub, I head into the kitchen, wearing my cozy bedroom slippers, and lift the kettle, shake it to see how much water is left from yesterday, plug it in. I am not concerned about germs in old water. I think I boil it often enough; besides, how can water matter? In the city it's chlorine and chemicals, in Ruth it's *E. coli*-whoever, the one that causes what the locals call beaver fever.

The kettle plugged in, I then reach for the filters for my Melitta pot. Sometimes they don't have size 102, which I am supposed to use, and then I buy size 2, which seems fine, although the cone is smaller. I think the Melitta people will be annoyed with me. It says right on each filter box, "Use the right size." I would like to write them, tell them I have always tried.

Filter in place, I open the refrigerator door and take out the can of Melitta coffee. I could get freshly ground beans, but I don't like coffee any more, and so am satisfied with the Melitta, which I recall as being good or at least good enough. Coffee measured in a heaping spoon, it waits bunched up for the water to scatter it, release its flavour.

I wait too. I still like the smell. The aroma, rather, of coffee brewing itself.

lambent

I hear the shouts of children exploding onto the play yard. Part of happiness is believing oneself alive, as the children in the play yard do. They don't question it, not for a moment! Look at the exuberance with which they run out of the building and how seriously they take their games, attacking one another full out, truth itself being defended. Believing that they matter. This belief, for me personally, has been the hardest of all to summon up routinely. But now, perhaps because of the clearer air in Ruth, the safety of a small residence inhabited by doddering elders of whom I am the "kid" in the crowd, only in my fifties, but no more popular for it, I know now who I am and why I am distinct and therefore exotic. I am privileged to know facts about myself that others aren't privy to about themselves, or else they ignore what tries to leak through consciousness, because they're afraid of being branded "different," or someone like me. I died in the fall of 1942 and was born in the spring of 1943. The best way to speak something so absurd is to announce it, as I've done. I died in a concentration camp somewhere in Poland, alone and separated from my real husband, whom I have never forgiven; I died alone and separated from my child.

But at last, in this new beginning, I sense I have located my lost boy. It is truly astonishing to me that he should turn out to be here in Ruth, of all places, where I, too, find myself. It is a miracle. I pick up my binoculars, lean eager thighs against the cool concrete confines of my terrace in order to steady myself. The boy is out in the windblown yard, near the fence. The others in his class are playing a chase game, directed by a foolish-looking, ruddy-faced man in baggy sweatpants. The look on the child's face is sad; he's starting to remember. I ache for all he has been through. He has a chameleon quality: his face phases through the fragility of early infancy to the hearty chubbiness of a child like Gil to the ghostly white of one forever dead. But he isn't, this boy is vibrantly alive, his eyes beautiful, deep and wild as every ocean I ever rested my gaze upon.

To me, he is the world. Today or tomorrow I will dress nicely, walk down the hill and present myself outside the play-yard fence and wait. And then, without my having to beckon him, but from some inner knowing, he will look up in recognition, wave, come to me.

FETISH

I.

WHAT HAPPENED THE SATURDAY morning Sue Ann opened the bathroom door by mistake and caught me apparently being a pervert — her word and not easy to use in relationship to myself — was, all hell broke loose in our trailer outside Cottonwood, Arizona. The Cottonwood area is at the flat end of an awesome canyon, a twenty-minute drive from Sedona, a country of red-rock outcroppings and scattered stands of pines and sunsets that have you, cold sober, doing wheelies in your mind. Thickets of cottonwoods grow along the river, like behind our place. Where we live the dust lying around the house is red. Any dampness and, bingo, it turns to clay.

Except for the odd time I've moved out and gone to live across the way with Clarissa, now the wife's best friend, Sue Ann and I have been together seven years. We came down as kids from the woods near Ruth, British Columbia, Canada, not South America (you have to tell people here basic crap like that), in a beat-up Chrysler of her dad's. Maybe I stole it, depends on your point of view. He was a bastard, had been doing his girls since Sue Ann was nine and her sister eleven. In a way I understood — high-mileage tits and clits being, like, everywhere in your face these days. But you can't forgive it when a dude gets off on kids old enough to remember, to feel the pain and remember, like Sue Ann and her sister.

Sue Ann's heart-stopping gasp, the sound of her inhaling the scene she'd interrupted in the john, fast-forwarded the memory of a childhood experience into the stuttering heartbeat of the present. Sue Ann's first shriek *singed* me. I came unglued. I didn't know where the hell I was. I was a five-year-old arsonist again and didn't know which way to run. I loved my mum; I'd done it for her. Match burning in my trembling fingers, I inched my bum along the well-worn pine-board floor closer to the hem of the summer skirt the dummy was wearing — the skirt my mother's first attempt at sewing and the cause, I understood, of her recent sadness. The diamond-bright beads of newborn flame ringed the hem of that skirt as though the nylon thread was dynamite powder, and as fast as a few blinks of the eye the skirt itself was going strong, the garish pink flowers on the pattern crinkling to black. Whole pieces shredded off in fiery flakes as the heat moved up the hips of the legless dummy. It was beautiful. It was fucking far-out, fantastically beautiful — until a screeching, thumping ruckus rushed towards what was by then a real blaze. I was kicked in the head and bulldozed flat. In the seconds before I blanked out, I saw Mum open her mouth. I saw her hoover in the flames. Then she reached out and whacked me.

In the closet-sized room smelling of baby poop, the wife, meanwhile, was going ballistic, knocking crap over, swatting at me. She was wearing an ugly muu-muu thing her sister sent from Waikiki. The howling, stuck in her throat, came out through clenched teeth and sounded like a high-speed drill. The eight-month-old twins, scared shit-less, gawked. She snatched one from where it was lying on the bathroom counter, the other from its carrier on the floor. They were bunched every which way in her arms, the bare-bummed boy upside down. I was quaking in my bones and fumbling to get my act together, tucking and zipping. The wife squeezed past and elbowed me in the gut. I saw spots, considered keeling over. The trailer rocked as the wife galloped down the hall. I heard both my little cuties overcome their shock and erupt into ear-wrenching wails. Them letting their fear rip shrank my balls to prunes. I was brought back to myself.

The wife is not a small person. She has this medium-long, thick Swedish-type hair that in good moods she uses Clairol on. The hair has a life of its own, living wild around her face, whose eyes have gone slitty from her putting on so much weight during the pregnancy. An Amazon type in general, Sue Ann could have taken me out in one punch. Yet when I made it to the living room she was cow-ering behind an end table, the one with Mr. Bowtie Bunny on it that I'd won for her at the Yavapai County Fair. The babies were raising the dead. Sue Ann was oblivious. Her gaze fixated itself on me like I was sprouting fur and fangs in front of her eyes.

"Shithouse mouse," I said. "Sue Ann, hon. Hey, pardner."

I tried more lovey-dovey claptrap. *Nada*. She had worked herself into a weirdly drowsy state of inner pandemonium that I was familiar with. She was staring. It was the kind of stare that could fool you into thinking somebody was asleep with their eyes open or else having a brain fit. I stepped closer and she snarled, a sound that has been known to pass her lips before; the wife is not your most stable person on the planet. I backed down, hands out like you do for the benefit of a mad dog, and bounded out of the place for Clarissa's.

Minus Clarissa over the years, I might have left Sue Ann, a karmically purposeless act — with my luck, I would just get born again and end up with quadruplets. Catching my breath in Clarissa's chaotic oasis with its overload of furniture, camera gear, books and dust balls was a relief. Louise, Clarissa's little girl, who was six and a general pain in the ass, was glaring at me from under a table. I've had to put up with her snark attacks since she was a crotchety baby. She was cutting up magazines for the second scrapbook of her future life, most of which so far looked like it was going to take place in the Arctic. She rolled her eyes at my groin, raised her scissors and went snip-snip. Louise goes around chanting, "Bobbitt, Bobbitt," like it's some kind of bird call.

Clarissa ignored her. She was on her knees, cutting a pattern spread on the floor. She was wearing rings and beads and a swirly batik skirt. Clarissa was a high-strung type totally dedicated to being super-cool. I was anxious to light a fire under her. I related the news that Sue Ann had gone apeshit and was maybe damaging the babies unconsciously.

Clarissa came through the door of our place like a Mack truck. By this time the babies were apoplectic and Sue Ann was wigged. Clarissa lifted one of the stone pendants she was wearing and used it to mesmerize the wife; she swung it back and forth, muttering something I didn't catch. My heart was in overdrive.

The wife's loony eyes flicked between Clarissa and me, then between her offspring like she was astonished she had them in her clutches. She passed the babies over to Clarissa, them screaming and grabbing at hair and air. These are heavyweights and they covered a lot of Clarissa's tight little bod, besides which in desperation they were flinging their clenched fists and landing a few. Clarissa tried handing them over to me. The wife panicked. She broke into strangulated sobs, between which she managed to bully me with some choice names, "pervert" and "rapist." Clarissa, burdened with babies, duck-walked over to the davenport and eased them — hell, more like chucked them — onto the cushions. They landed in an enraged heap.

She turned and told me to keep my distance. I did. This event was becoming as embarrassing as pissing into a strong wind. The women moved into the kitchen, within earshot, keeping an eye on me like my debased nature would drive me to perform some slime-bucket number on the twins right then and there. Neither the wife nor Clarissa twigged to my philosophy of the thing. They didn't get that I loved the babies, the major joy they bring — from the whiff of their skin after a bath to licking a tear from their cheek to make them forget their little troubles.

It's simple. There's ways you can get loving using a baby that don't, in my opinion, make you a degenerate doing it. The wife, she tells you, "Go change the baby, hon"; and maybe it's been a while and you get a kind of itch thinking about the little bugger. You start salivating over its soft, teeny parts, but the thing is, you don't harm it by poking yourself or anything else into it. Boy or girl, you get your pleasure by laying them out and mesmerizing yourself by staring at them, inspecting them, letting the desire grow for the fruit inside them that *you cannot have*. This last bit I'm totally clear on. If the wife wants to know "What's taking so long, hon?" I just say the baby spit up and I'm cleaning it off; or hell, I felt like giving the sweet little sucker a bath, giving the wife a break, anything that pops into my head that makes sense, domestically speaking.

This has sort of been my philosophy. My fooling around is not a big deal; I don't do damage to them by hurting or threatening or any of that sick shit. Most of the time I don't even lay a finger on them. Babies don't remember and what you don't remember can't hurt you.

This is how I was thinking, listening to the women dissect me. I admit it was kind of riveting, sitting cross-legged on the floor — near enough to the davenport so I could reach an arm out if the rollicking ankle-biters bounced themselves off — listening to the wife laying her charges against me, hearing myself spoken of like I was some really heavy dude. I was getting a whole new angle on a life I'd thought of as being your basic. Unfortunately, as Sue Ann went on, Clarissa, who'd given up on men and was thinking of becoming lesbian, began to eye me like you would some stinking road kill.

Babies have a way of getting on with life. Women don't. Instead, women have a destructive, inbred desire to get to the bottom of things. Sue Ann did come to her senses about calling the police, but her and Clarissa both wanted to take a *proactive* stance to the situation. Clarissa's screwy idea was that we should see somebody at the Celestial Center for the New Age, in Sedona. It being a Saturday, the Center had various freelancers on hand. Who she had in mind was a deep-trance channeller named Baba Jhon who specialized in past-life therapy. He had the rep for harmonizing hard cases. We needed to gain insight into the karmic indicators that had led to the travesty. That was Clarissa talking.

At the Center half an hour later, I followed Clarissa inside to take a leak while she negotiated with Duane Dewitt, the dude who called himself Baba Jhon. He didn't look like much: skinny, like me, maybe even shorter, but with a pile of golden hair that made me check it out twice. Then Clarissa and I waited on a bench outside a room in the back of the shop while the wife had some time alone with him, saying God knew what. I broke into a sweat. What you do inside your own privacy was beginning to feel like a totally different matter when gaped upon through the eyes of another consciousness. I heard Sue Ann sob. "What the hell," I said. Clarissa reached out her hand — the one with the knobby middle knuckle that she broke on a wall, trying to punch me out once — and eased open the door.

They were sitting at a round table covered in a lacy white cloth, holding hands, which they eased off doing when we went in. Three utility candles burned in the centre of the table, along with a stick of smouldering incense musking up the windowless space. The baba indicated some chairs. Sue Ann turned to Clarissa. She said, "It's karma, all right. Heavy, like you wouldn't believe." In my direction, without meeting my eyes, she said, "You might have been my father in another life. We were gypsies in the thirteenth century — the thirteenth, is that right?" She gave the baba a look. He touched her hand and nodded. "Yeah," went Sue Ann, like a bolt of energy'd hit her, "and marauders came and attacked our wagon and raped and wasted my mother and tried to rape me, but you stepped in and with your sabre you slayed them and protected me. In payment, I've had to bow down to you and obey you."

"To a point," Baba Jhon said.

"To a point." The wife laid a quick, conspiratorial smile on him. She continued talking, frowning at me, like she'd memorized the spiel. "If you actually hurt my babies, I might be destined to kill you. It's a mother's responsibility."

The baba knew us intimately; he knew so well the life the wife and I had shared he could have been a flea in our gypsy wagon. A voice with a heavy accent rose from Sue Ann's head and thanked me for saving her, and then Clarissa burst into tears. She said, "I was the wife you didn't save. You rescued our daughter instead of me." I knew from the electricity moving through me that her words were true. It explained our defaulted relationship.

The three of them went back and forth on whether the babies were the incarnated marauders and that was why I had this unconscious desire to, like, *degrade* them. It was a sicko theory. To my mind, the babies were innocence itself.

"Bullshit," I muttered.

"You've suffered humiliation many lifetimes," the baba said.

Bullshit, I tried to say again, but my lips were glued. The room overheated. An entity began talking above my head or behind my back or maybe inside my brain — I underwent some clammy, muddled moments. It turned out the baba had more spirits plugged into him than a cat had lives. A leaden sadness fell on my heart. When the room grew quiet I opened my eyes to find the baba gazing at me.

In the dream I was trapped in a forest. The events are confused by fire raging in trees that are red like the desert whizzing past the car heading home to Cottonwood. I was tucked awkwardly in one corner of the back seat, Sue Ann in the other, us separated by canvas bags ripped off from the post office, stuffed with Clarissa's clothes and crap. The burning trees are angry at me, ablaze in their anger because I'm born wrong, "gen-u-ine-ly goddamn dumb," Pop used to say, acting ignorant when he wasn't. I'm in a partial clearing, scared shitless, surrounded by a ring of burning trees smelling of cedar from my childhood. Just as I figure I'm toast, a mystical opening appears, an escape route, a road. I start forward and then a truck, a logging truck, comes rumbling right at me, its high beams on.

Clarissa's vehicle stank like B-vitamins, mildewed tent, maybe some granola gone rancid. It was packed with stuff, front and back, because when she felt screwed mentally, she'd head out to the canyons for a few days, us or the Guatemalan babysitter looking after Louise. I was bummed out about remembering the dream when so much else, all the lives and sadness, was churning in my brain like a bellyful of undercooked pinto beans. Then Sue Ann, with her perfect timing, remarked out of the blue, "I think we should call the police." As though we hadn't just been through a spiritual wringer of under-standing and sharing.

"I'm the one that has to do the exchange," Clarissa said. She was ticked off because we owed Baba Jhon thirty dollars and Sue Ann had volunteered one of Clarissa's cool massages. The baba was a hard bargainer; she'd have to put in a whole hour. "And it's you he liked. He never held *my* hand."

"What does that have to do with anything?" the wife asked.

"It's not my asshole old man got us in this mess."

To divert them, I said, "Something stinks in this car."

"*You're* in it, Bobby," said the helpmeet.

"Hold on. Christ's sake. You heard the baba. I suffered plenty in my time. There are *reasons*."

"Yeah, there are reasons, yeah right, I got that, but I been thinking and while the baba makes sense, what I see is that some prick has been trying to rape me forever, every fucking life, and I also see what you're doing is rape."

She wound down, sinking into her spacy stare. I knew she was stuck in a zombie zone by her dad and what he did. Looking at her made me want to bawl like some kind of baby myself. Sue Ann's body was puffy, the way of somebody chronically pigging out at McDonald's. It was true, she's addicted to the fish sandwich loaded with mayonnaise, she'll eat four at a sitting. But it's because she's bursting with sadness. When I'm on top, and we're doing it, I can feel a million tears welling on the inward side of her skin.

" — even if you're not in them," she concluded, oblivious that she'd vanished from her sentence. She had this bewildered look when she turned to me. Her eyes were a washed-out hazel and kind of blended into her so-so features and frizzy hair, as though her physical self never wanted anybody to notice her or single her out for anything ever again.

Fugue states made me nervous. I decided to justify my actions, a mistake I continually make in this life. "What I do is harmless, hon. A tension releaser, you know? Like stress? They don't even know it."

"Yeah, well, they don't know it maybe" — this woman could rally a deep-seated belligerence at the drop of a hat — "but it's some kind of rape, I got this feeling, and those are my babies and you are somehow *doing* them."

"*Our* babies."

"I'm the one has to do the exchange," said Clarissa.

"Hey, hon, I'm a *survivor*," I pointed out, reasonable as all hell.

"Yeah, well, *I'm* a survivor," Sue Ann retorted.

"Everybody who's not dead is a survivor," said Clarissa. "When you think about it." Her foot was pretty heavy on the gas pedal as she made up her mind to pass a U-Haul.

She took her eyes off the road, riveted us through the rearview mirror. "What you smell is partly mice. Their nest's back there in one of those bags." She knew Sue Ann's phobia, how she'd freak at small, furry creatures; we couldn't even have a kitten. Introducing the topic of mice in a car with Sue Ann in it was epically suicidal.

Clarissa passed sixty miles an hour and the Pontiac, balding tires out of alignment, did its usual wobble trip, rear end skewing. It was like she was taking the ultimate dare, testing karma and fate to the limit. Like she'd decided we deserved to go up in flames for our sins or whatever. Clarissa was raised a strong Catholic. It's their mind's second nature to groove on guilt at untimely moments.

I saw a red pick-up bombing directly at us in the other lane. The U-Haul hunched over towards the shoulder. "Mice," Clarissa said in the rearview, staring straight at the wife. Somebody was laying on a horn. The wife was starting a panic attack. Her chest went rigid, her breathing irregular. Me, I detached from the scene. I was like gone. My whole life was a dream. The dream had been about my death all along.

We went through what seemed like a wind tunnel. When the shuddering stopped, the pick-up had passed and Clarissa was sailing ahead of the U-Haul. The sun shone on the ridges to the west. The sky was the lilac blue of a desert afternoon. A hawk spiralled slowly down a current of air. My brain was totally silenced, a concept I don't often experience.

Clarissa slammed on the brakes, yanked the Pontiac off the road and came to a slewing stop. Suddenly I tuned in that she was shouting, her face contorted and uncool. She was shouting something about her clothes. In a daze I looked over and saw Sue Ann busily tossing stuff out the window, reaching into the laundry bags in a frenzy. Bare-handed. Brave.

I was gaping at this beauty action of the wife's when she wasn't there, Clarissa wasn't there, the two of them were outside the car jumping at each other, tugging at each other's hair, fair game for tourist cameras or anybody else bored with their own life. It was amazing: them scuffling sand, puffing up a storm, grunting, cursing, Clarissa fast, small and reckless, Sue Ann slow, canny, in for the long haul. Jeez, *women*, was all I could think.

I collected myself enough to drag the two laundry bags from the car into the landscape. I emptied them next to a teddy-bear cholla. When the nest of hairless pink mice showed up tangled in Clarissa's underwear, I stomped them, the idea being that I was protecting my woman. That she would see my reaction as siding with her, against Clarissa, in whatever was going on between them.

A tiny, piercing squealing rose over the rougher sounds of traffic and them skirmishing. The women stopped their tussling like they'd been electrocuted. They turned as one — you'd have thought they were joined at the hip — and checked out what had gone down.

"God in heaven," the wife said, ogling the bloody nest and then me.

The one that must have been the mother zipped in frantic circles, squeaking, around the mess of what had been her babies. I looked at the bottoms of my boots. I thought I might heave.

As we drove past the boulders of red rock and some weedy desert crap with a pink plastic flamingo stuck in the centre that marked the entrance to Cottonwood Trailer Park, Sue Ann, who'd been thinking hard, said, "I think we should talk to Louise."

Clarissa parked the Pontiac in her space. "Holy Mother," she breathed.

In unison we got out of the car. "No way," I said, following behind. "No way, swear to God."

Sue Ann brought Louise from our place and walked her out of earshot of the babysitter, watching from behind the screen door, holding one of my babies, probably the girl, who was alert to the action. The boy, being male, tended to sleep more.

Clarissa knelt and took Louise's hand. Clarissa had this dramatic nature often thwarted by real life. She did a preamble number about self-esteem, the rights of the child, boundaries and integrity, all that pop-psych puke. Louise was bored out of her gourd. Waiting for Clarissa to finish, for entertainment she twitched her nose, practising her rabbit imitation, which she was pretty good at.

Patience wasn't Sue Ann's long suit and she cut to the chase. "Listen, Louise, what we want to know is, did Bobby ever touch you funny? Stick his fingers up your panties, anything creepy like that?"

Louise had a trickster mentality and a mean streak a mile wide. Enough to make anybody nervous. Staring past the dilapidated washhouse towards the creek, I started whistling, attempting to chill out. Then I thought back. Louise might remember the whistling from when I was distracting her. The whistling might trigger some memory that ought to stay buried. I wasn't a fucking monster.

She was small-boned, a dwarf in a little yellow print cotton shift, tanned legs skinny, birdlike feet bare in the red dirt. She stepped in front of the two women and faced me. Her eyes slid coyly in my direction. This behaviour would be just like Louise, to toy with her victim when she knew she had him by the shorties. I broke into a sweat. Clarissa would kill me.

Something was weird in what Louise was up to, weirder than the usual Louise. She was doing some bashful number, spots of colour blotching her cheeks as she blinked one eye, then the other — she didn't know how to wink yet, she was still working on it. Then it hit me. She was trying to *flirt* with me.

Jesus.

She smiled this beauty smile of seeming innocence and turned towards the women. "He might've," she said.

"There's a hole there, all right." She did her cute-kid twirly hop. Sue Ann reached out her hand. I heard a roar in my head. I thought I would go blind or pass out from the brilliant pain crashing into my skull.

II.

WOMEN DRIVE YOU CRAZY with their empowerment trips, like this goddess thing Clarissa got the wife into. They have been at it every day for over two weeks. It created in me a very ticked-off emotion, thinking about the wife worshipping some big-bellied, droopy-titted earth mother that's better than what men have. I was careful around Sue Ann, though, who has a volatile personality. Most I would say was "How's the hummingbird egg holding up? Hatched yet?" in reference to one of the items of nature they have on the shrine over there. Sometimes I could hear them thrumming like bullfrogs in heat, singing and beating drums. Me and everybody else in Cottonwood Trailer Park, outside Cottonwood, Arizona, home of red dust and dirty feet in crappy Chinese sandals from K-Mart. This last factor I was noticing while pushing my twin babies in their wagon for a twilight outing. I'd rigged the unit myself: them strapped in their baby seats and the seats strapped to the wagon with rope, wire and whatever else I scavenged at the trash. Tonight the dotty old lady, her white hair looking electrocuted, is standing in the lane, like she's waiting for us, hubby keeping an eye on her from behind a crack in the drapes. She asks me how old the babies are. She wants to touch their soft cheeks and I let her. She gets this weirdly sad look as the backs of her fingers stroke their faces. Then she asks me again how old they are. It's like a mantra she's into.

I push on, thinking about how Clarissa was bad news in that she was a leader against the status quo. The three of us — Clarissa, Sue Ann and me — have been entangled in an unhealthy manner for years. The women think the reason is some weird karma trip. Due to recent events, I had become the enemy, representing the evils of mankind, meaning men.

Or rather, as the wife said, "It isn't you, exactly, Bobby. It's your hormones and their bad instincts that are stimulated by our decadent society. You and your penis are just users, out for power trips, but it's not your fault, exactly. You are a victim of the invading patriarchal culture that took over around 5000 B.C. It has something to do with horses." Sue Ann has this way of talking. She goes along pretty impressively and then her face screws up in a frown and she pops out something from left field and wanders off.

When I get back after the outing — my baby girl whimpering from a dog encounter and the boy sound asleep — that brat Louise comes sashaying across the tarmac, wearing a dress she has obviously handmade herself. The dress is two rectangles of white muslin sheet that she's sewed at the shoulders and down the sides in loopy running stitches. She's wearing it over a pair of red shorts. She watches me struggle to unhook the girl from my contraption, but she doesn't lift a finger. It would be helpful if she held the wagon so the snoozing little fellow wouldn't get banged in the head from the tussle going on between me and his stiff-legged sister. But no. "I'm not allowed to get too close to you," Louise says. "You know why, too, you pervert."

Louise and I have always had a not-hundred-per-cent relationship. "Blow it out your ear," I tell her automatically, ducking as my baby girl flails a tiny fist. She's got her cross-eyed look, a bad sign; she has the hot-and-cold personality of her mother. Sweat is dripping off me as I race up the trailer's wobbly stairs, open the screen door, set the girl on the floor on the far side of the room, shut the door quick, hop down again and begin unstrapping the boy.

"You ain't supposed to get close to me." Louise has these fierce chocolate-bead eyes and a ferret face. As a baby she had some potential in the looks department.

"Your mom don't let you say 'ain't.'"

"Yeah, right, that's what you think." Louise is still at me, irrational as a blackfly. I heave the boy over my shoulder, where he settles like a damp puppy. His eyes flutter open. He smiles at some sweet dream. Man, this is one beautiful kid. I get off on the sweetness of my babies.

The girl has got over to the door and is staring at us through the screen. Louise takes a step closer. She says, "Look what I got." She flashes her hand and there's a polished stone figure, the one that a man can hardly escape from these days. No head, just boobs and belly. Despite the girl baby figuring to bust through the door, I reach out my hand. The object is sweaty from Louise's mitt. It's made of a green rock and has a nice weight. When I look up, Louise is gone like an evil fairy, and I am left staring at the thing like I've never seen a pair of boobs before. I tuck it in my pocket and trundle up the rickety stairs, thinking about getting the babies some supper.

Friday night the women did a full-moon tree-hug down by the riverbed. Afterwards, our lives took a dive, worse than usual. I got a non-stop, coast-to-coast headache. With my head in pain, my dreams got bad, the fire I sometimes re-experience roaring in my cells again. The weather was so hot the fans made no difference, we were all like dried pinto beans in a tin can, even the babies were deadbeats.

When I brought up with Clarissa the situation of the childhood fire recurring in my brain, she said it was my conscience awakening and hallelujah. This was not the analytical, sympathetic Clarissa I was used to. She had a leaner, meaner look in her eye. She'd changed. They all had changed. Even the girl baby started the trick of turning her face away when I went to kiss her.

Underestimating the power of a female has always been my mistake. There's something about them that seems weak under the surface, like they have some unfinished trauma held back. Meanwhile I was tiptoeing around, being helpful to Sue Ann around the house, easing her way, but to no avail. The following Tuesday, she up and decides to move over to Clarissa's. I get home from the grocery store, bringing a special treat for her, Redenbacher's Movie Popcorn. Buying the popcorn was definitely my intuition at work but the gesture is too late: there she is, halfway through the door, one hand hefting a suitcase and under her arm a baby. "Get a job, Bobby," she says.

At first I was relatively calm. I phoned over but they hung up on me. Cool. I could dig it, I would bide my time. I knew the women would be bickering despite the sisterhood shit; Clarissa's place was only a two-bedroom single-wide and my and Sue Ann's babies, although nine months old, have never slept through a single night. Clarissa was employed at a healing centre in Sedona as a part-time administrator, which meant she was making an effort to show up in ironed clothes.

A man grows lonely with only the sound of his own farting to keep him company. As the days went by, I was milling and stewing and feeling more and more like a trip to the store was too hard to mobilize for. I kept my self-respect by mopping the kitchen floor and taking out the trash on time and opening cans of Chunky Choice soup and making myself eat it. At night from across the way I heard my babies giving the world hell, their voices raised in tandem screeching. They made me proud.

What I wanted, what I really wanted more than free cold beer, was Sue Ann saying some routine rude thing to me and a gurgling wet-diapered baby or two to bounce on my knee. It's that kind of image which sticks in your brain as being the ideal domestic life you used to lead, whether you did or not.

I have a belief that life takes you along on its own current and you haven't much choice how the flow goes. I
would rather have been a dude who gets into alcohol in a
big way and spends his waking hours grieving face down
in a toilet bowl than the subtler type of sinner that I was,
not black, not white, some mouldy shade of grey. Taking
my babies away from me like that, the women had me
pinned like a cockroach to a wall. I got to thinking of
human rights and other basic crap: women and children
packed like sardines, holed up, braving it out just to keep
away from me. It was pitiful. So I did the only humanitar-
ian thing: I phoned Sue Ann and told her to bring the
babies on home, I would leave. Making the phone call felt
good. I could feel rising in me a virtual righteousness, that
for once I was making a noble move.

So I packed and sat on the step waiting for her to come
out and thank me or say goodbye, but there wasn't a sign
of life over there. Clarissa has these rubber-backed drapes
to keep the sun out, that you buy from the Sears catalogue
store or also the Wal-Mart in Flagstaff carries them. The
rubber's shredded in places, like insects were at it. I kept
watch, waiting even for that pill Louise to give me her
tongue. *Nada.* I had sort of thought Sue Ann would come
to her senses and beg me to stay, but obviously Clarissa had
her tied down or something, wanting her peaceful life
back. Clarissa has a selfish streak a mile wide.

I hitch into Sedona, carrying the taped-up Samsonite
and wearing a backpack, fingering the goddess in my
pocket every chance I get. At the Celestial Center for the

New Age, I ask for our old channeller pal, Duane Dewitt, who channels the entity called Baba Jhon. He's not in but will be a week Sunday, but, man, no way can I wait that long. The girl behind the counter has these incredible turquoise eyes like maybe she's wearing coloured contacts, and when I bring up her incredible eyes, she turns cold on me. Women usually see my good qualities right off, but there's a new batch these days that must have suckled serious attitude directly from the tit.

I have this urge to see Baba Jhon. I want to talk man to man with the dude, find out more about the past lives that led me to here. I head to the corner gas station and in the phone booth go through the pages until I find it. Dewitt on Wayfarer's Road. *Perfecto mundo*. I take a bus along 89A and then walk west, into the sun. By now the heat of the day has peaked.

Wayfarer's Road is paved only to the point of an abandoned church, a dirty adobe affair with broken windows and graffiti on the walls. It stinks inside, vomit and shit. The road then disintegrates into a rock-strewn, red-dust trail. My moustache is a mop, collecting dust.

I walk into the sunset forever, the knapsack cutting into my right shoulder, the strap frayed. The road peters out and there's a decent house, adobe with a brick-coloured tile roof, that rises like hope itself. The crotch-high fence around the yard is constructed of woven twigs and branches. Inside the yard, which is swept dirt, white-painted rocks form designs around a few ordinary cacti. There's one stunning ocotillo, its bundle of wavy, prickly blades high as the house. When I was just down from B.C., where there's real trees with leaves and bark, I used to sneer at ocotillo, they were so dopey looking. But now I see them as necessary desert outbursts, like thin-armed crazy men praying for rain, craving water or maybe just wanting to be noticed, both feelings I am fully simpatico with. My throat is beyond dry. It's starting to come back to me that the baba did not find me especially likeable. I open the latch and step inside the compound. I am careful to close the gate, to keep out whatever it is Duane Dewitt doesn't want in.

A girl answers the door, she's part Spanish or Indian with skin the colour of tanned leather and big olive-green eyes. She checks me out, kind of looks not directly at me but around me like she can see my aura. She nods me in. The house is whitewashed, cool, terracotta tile floors, Indian rugs scattered around. Baba Jhon has good taste. She — her name is Graciella — lets me wash the dust and heat off my face and sits me at the formica table in the kitchen, and after I chug back about a quart of water, she pours me some barley coffee substitute, lukewarm from a pot on a back burner. It is awful-tasting shit that tends to give me the runs but I don't want to be rude. The kitchen smells of tomato and cilantro and simmering fatty pork. She's making tamales. I watch her spoon red chile sauce into the centre of the shredded meat that she then dabs into the warm masa meal, her little fingers quick as she builds each tamale and wraps it in its corn husk. Then she packs them into a cooler. She's a fast talker, chit-chit like a ground squirrel, her English not too smooth. She's from the Taos Pueblo and even though she's part Mexican, a language called Tiwa, she tells me, is her real talk. Duane is on the road, channelling his way through Phoenix, Tucson and Yuma. He's been gone ten days, which I figure explains her chattering; she's real alone out here. She's making the tamales to sell at a pueblo fair over in New Mexico.

I ease into the smell of the kitchen, the cool comfort of being with a nice woman, one that's not crazy into goddess shit or severe judgement.

When the last of the batch is in the cooler, she washes her hands and turns to me. She then performs a mind-blowing action, takes her time running her hands down her small, pointed breasts inside the white peasant blouse splattered with bits of sauce, takes her time along her square midriff, across her rounded belly and down to her thighs. It is a turn-on, big time. "I am three months with child," she says. "Knocked up." She giggles.

I want to go for her, but I am also super-attuned to the fact that there is no joy in the sound she makes. I can't resist myself, I push aside the chair and walk towards her and gather her in my arms, my hands making their way along her firm back to grab and hold her chubby ass. What I am projecting is not disrespectful. She starts to cry. "Duane is not marrying me," she says against my chest. "And I am Catholic."

Women have got it rough, getting used by guys as sex objects until the crunch. I at least married Sue Ann.

Duane Dewitt is supposed to be a holy dude. Still holding her, I ask myself why I assume a channeller is holy — they're not priests or anything, not that being a priest means much any more, what with the kiddy scandals — and meanwhile all this thinking makes me rest my cheek on the top of her head and breathe in the eucalyptus shampoo and oil of her hair and give a deep sigh, and she does the same against me, and we are just standing holding each other in this kitchen that because of her work smells melt-in-your-mouth. Tears fill my eyes. I say, "I'll marry you, just say the word," and she giggles again, and this time she's happy.

I believe in instant karmic events between people, and between Graciella and me is one of those zones of rapport. So I stay and help out — wash some walls, scrape paint off a rocking chair she wants for the baby. When Duane isn't back, at dawn on Thursday she gets the pick-up from out behind the garage — the garage full of furniture like from somebody's suburban nightmare garage sale, rotting orange davenports and yellowed lampshades on broken stands and brown loopy rugs — and we pack up, head north, the cooler full of tamales bouncing in the back, take 40 into Gallup, sailing through the Petrified Forest, stopping for Cokes in Houck, into New Mexico, bypass Albuquerque, pull off, follow a road to where the party is. I am by now hazy about my whole past life as I unstick myself from the seat — Graciella drives like a born westerner, flat out — into the sound of a live Peruvian band and the sight of rows of tarp-covered booths selling blankets and black-velvet paintings and turquoise trinkets to people of all colours milling about.

Graciella sets up the cook stove in the back of the truck, starts boiling water in a pot. I wander around, stuff myself on Indian fry bread and candied cactus, corn roasted on the fire. Graciella's tamales sell well, especially to the guys in the band. Everybody thinks this beauty chick is mine and they're cool around her. She's wearing a cotton dress with flowers on it and laughing and smiling, eyes the colour of sage in springtime. Once, watching her out of the corner of my eye, I realize that I don't miss anybody when I'm looking at her.

We're camping in a tent out behind the rec centre where, besides normal bureaucracy, they've got counselling and sex education crafts, like condoms wrapped in felt valentines the girls make to give to their boyfriends. Actually Graciella's in the tent and I'm outside like a guard dog, lying on a dried-up foamy, tucked into Duane's mummy bag. Because she's Catholic, right. But earlier we spent some time sitting in the tent, cross-legged and facing each other, the lantern making her dark face even more mysterious. She says to me, "Feel. This is God, making," and takes my hand and lowers it to press the off-centre lump. I think my trouble is just beginning. All Sue Ann did while pregnant was barf and swear.

Duane Dewitt himself arrives home on Saturday. I'm camped on his enclosed porch, wrapped in a sheet, having a siesta. Him talking loud to Graciella like she's deaf, while he's rooting around in the refrigerator, looking for something to eat is what wakes me, and then he glances up, squinting like a bear catching a scent. My being conscious triggers the reaction of alertness in him, which is pretty far out. My heart starts racing a bit, remembering his good-looking face, his shock of blond hair, his aura of charisma and how calm he was handling me and Sue Ann's weird trip. I untangle myself from the sheet and stand, planning an old-buddy greeting. He slams the fridge door so that Graciella's ceramic Lady of Sorrow tumbles off and thuds to the floor. "Who is that?" he asks her, grabbing her arm.

"It is a friend," she says. "It is a friend is all. Bobby."

"Bobby? Oh, it's *Bobby*."

"Yeah, hey man," I start mumbling, tucking in my shirt.

"*That* Bobby," he says. "Sure, come on in, buddy boy." His eyes never leave her.

"Hey, thanks, man," I enthuse and get two steps into the kitchen before the channeller decks me.

When I come to, I'm propped on the couch in the living room and he's leaning over me with a grin on his face. "Sorry, pal," he says. "She's good in the sack, wouldn't you agree?" I can't make out his point, except when I catch on that he's still *watching* her. "Unusual for an Indian. Really totally un-Catholic, wouldn't you agree?"

It's the repeating the "wouldn't you agree" business that makes me think the guy is wacko. Sort of like the wife, Sue Ann, who gets zombied, but this, it feels more on the dangerous side. He has a loonier glint in his eye — just one, I notice, the right one — than Sue Ann ever managed in both of hers. I ease up, slow, so as not to disturb the rattler lurking in his nature, move my legs to make sure they work, reach my hand slowly around to straighten a pillow behind my back.

"I only protected her," I say.

My remark gives him another idea, one that I didn't intend. "Those Indians try to get at her?"

"No, hey, no way, man, she's loyal like a dog to you." I was sorry calling anything about Graciella doglike but I was feeling desperate. There was a newness in my ability to sense danger. Either that or my paranoia was progressing faster than normal. I change the subject. "I was your slave in another life. The Roman life. I wouldn't do anything to harm you. You treated me decent."

This tack also is not a good idea. "You say. Maybe you're after revenge, maybe revenge is messing with my woman. What lurks in the human heart is weightier than most mortals can comprehend. Deeper. You might not even know why the hell you came here. Motivated by an inner urging your ordinary, low-level intelligence doesn't twig to, thinking you just want to pay the wise man a visit. Knowing on the vibrational level he's not even in town. Knowing his woman is lonely. Moving in on her susceptibilities, using your boyishness, which is really, by the way, totally out of keeping with your age, you really should get on with it — " Here he loses his train of thought, pondering my personality weaknesses. "How do

I know what you're doing? How do I know you are who you say you are?"

"Oh, it's me all right, Bobby, Bobby Fauler. Me and the wife and Clarissa — you recall Clarissa? Massage?" Then I shut up, too late for my own good. Because he does remember, and he didn't before.

"Ah," he breathes; the burp after the mouse is a mere bump in the belly of the snake. He hiccups with laughter, bending over, reaching for Graciella, who has a half-smile on her face, anxious for him to be happy, anxious that he is. She steps under his right arm and he pulls her face close. It's me he's watching now, holding her uncomfortably tight, suppressing giggles is what he's doing, moving his head, listening to what me and Graciella can't hear, eyeing me again. "Shucks, Gracie," he says. "This is the man who gets off on babies. This dude masturbates on his *babies*. They were, what, six months old? Seven?" He laughs loud and Graciella, after a shocked pause, struggles out of his grasp, wiggling herself free. I close my eyes, cringing, unable to bear what's starting on her face, how appalling this news is to her — and it is appalling, the idea of someone getting off on babies, hearing it cold from a terrible, evil person like Duane. I am sucked into a vacuum. Then I hear her bare feet hit the floor, hear a door slam, hear Duane wheezing his laughter down, feel his hand on my arm. I brush him away. He sits beside me, his heavier weight on the soft cushions pulling me towards him.

"Sorry, old pal, I thought you would have told her.

174

I thought you two were *friends*, you know, like you were saying."

There's a silence, then I hear a gasp from the other room, picture Graciella face into a pillow. I open my eyes and look at Duane. He grins at me, and he's transformed back into a mellow guy.

"Buck up now, truth is always better than no truth." Something about this makes him laugh. "I've got a joint." He places his arm around my shoulder, his fist touching my throat. It's a hammerlock, basically. Neither of us moves, although I hear his breathing in my right ear. I feel like five years old and dropping. He senses some giving up in me at the same moment I actually do it. I just sit there, looking at my useless, uncallused hands.

"Okay," he says, something resolved. He moves, pulls up a chair, lights up. We solemnly pass the joint back and forth, me getting zonked quick, both of us listening to the woman crying in the bedroom. Duane is smiling sadly, once in a while his tongue making a regretful clicking sound. "Boy oh boy, boy oh boy," he says, and I nod and he shakes his head and I can only figure that the world is a cuckoo place. I touch my chin where he slugged me. "You didn't intend anything bad," he says. "I'm getting that my guides are telling me you didn't mean any harm coming here."

"I didn't. I'd never hurt her."

"That serious, huh." Duane leans forward, studying me with interest. "Tell you what," he says, rising. "Come on. I got some magic out back you need."

175

I follow him through the kitchen — automatically picking up the unbroken statue and putting it on the counter — and out into the yard. The space isn't really a yard, exactly, a wire fence around a section of desert. He has a great view of some layered red-rock buttes, and because his land is situated like it is, no houses directly next door, it's dark except for the lights from his house and so the stars are clear, the Milky Way shooting past, whooshing back and forth in this awesome arc right over our heads.

"Far out," says Duane, his strong hand taking hold of my wrist and leading me somehow out past the fence further into the desert, the lights from his house and the others way in the distance mere flickers. I realize he's a shaman and not necessarily a light-based one, but his powers I have to respect, they're holy, and I ought to pay homage or at least pay attention. Well, yeah, I think I ought to pay attention, like wondering where the hell am I and why does my head hurt so bad and who is this guy I can't even see any more, who is walking around me chanting things I don't understand. I only think he's walking around me because I feel his energy but my eyes won't focus on him, that is, if any part of him except his voice — which I for sure hear — is even physically present. For all I know he has turned into a bat and is flying around the distant butte in a covey or however bats do when they hang out. The goddess in my pocket is throbbing against my thigh. This idea sends a shiver through me. I think the shit he had me smoke was weird.

There's a blank where I don't know what happened next, except I wake up on the patio and Graciella is making the barley coffee in the kitchen and she's humming, which in my book means he probably plugged her good, which probably I should have had the balls to do, after all, since he figured I did and she hates me anyway. Duane is first to notice me struggling to get up and steps out and claps me on the shoulder. "Eggs? Bacon? Toast, maybe?" I am obviously befuddled because what goes through my brain is basic, like why anybody who eats eggs and bacon would drink that fake coffee crap, and I would give an arm and a leg for some real brew. Like I'm not thinking anything deeper but am getting the sense of the brushoff. Eat and run, Duane's final pat on my shoulder conveys. His friendly pat has enough strength in it to jog my headache loose. "Oh, hell," I say and wince in his direction. I see the dude did it on purpose and maybe my life would last longer if indeed I hightailed it out of there.

Full of eggs and bacon and refried beans, I get to the door, Samsonite taped shut with new tape and my backpack weighing me down in my weakened condition, Graciella disappearing after plunking down the plate in front of me, when Duane calls after me: "Oh, hey, buddy, give me your address. We should keep in touch, we've been through so much together." I give him the address in Cottonwood — what the hell, it's not like I live there any more — and then turn my back on it all, Graciella that I'm in love with despite my head-splitting pain and him, my master and guru and something bad news, too. Nemesis. Clarissa's word for me.

I hate being dirty and not able to shower at least every second day and I hate begging food money — strangers look at you like you're going to buy booze, for one thing, and the other folks, the ones you know (which suddenly seems like just about everybody — me and Sue Ann have done survival gigs all over the area), tease you about being given the door by the wife. Domestic news travels like wildfire. The third day into lacking a domestic cover and I am starting to look bad, some innocence I was so good at lost. My long curly hair is straggly, my eyes are haggard and underlined. I don't sleep, even the night an old gal takes me in and lets me use her spare-room cot. She does it because she remembers what a nice waiter I was at La Splendido, where she came every night for Manhattans and dinner the month her husband left her.

Being in that spare room makes me feel like a kid, a feeling that while I do not like it, I do admit to cherishing certain aspects of it, like people doing things for you because you're helpless. I used to make my brother Matthew open the cans for dinner, even though I'd figured how to use the can opener myself. I'd sit dejected at the kitchen table, fiddling with a spoon, until he broke down. The spare room reminds me of Mum's, the spare room in our rented house on J Avenue with its one scraggly cedar out front, the house before Ian McDougall became our step-pop and took over our lives. It was a throw-all room: our outgrown bikes, the photo albums, Mum's sewing machine that mostly didn't work but sometimes did, a busted typewriter from when she thought she'd learn to type, the cot me or Matthew was sent to if we fought too much in our room — she wouldn't give over the spare, she said brothers were supposed to share memories — her pile of library books, always overdue, shoeboxes being saved for mailing something in and short curtains with blue bows along the top and dusty fake-oak panel board on all the walls. Matthew's still in Ruth, being a slave at Ian's funky resort, doing what the man tells him. Him being such a wimp makes me sigh.

I can't get to sleep for the wind that keeps blowing through my bones, raising goose bumps in my flesh. I think of Graciella and the ease between us, the Indian thing of patience and peacefulness woven into her being, like she is an ancient basket despite the short-shorts and her trying to cook "white" for Duane. When things went haywire, like when I busted the bathtub handle trying to fix the leak or her yeast bread didn't rise, she took things philosophically, nodding and smiling, "Yup, yup." Shrugging and starting all over or going to lie outside. She didn't use any chaise-longue crap, she'd lie on her back on the swept dirt and spread her arms, embracing the sun. The dirt on the surface of her hair was never dirty dirt, just kind of the clean, groomed kind. Where Sue Ann is a Nordic goddess, Graciella is an earth mother, formed out of that soil she lay on.

Thinking of Graciella makes me toss and turn and the cot squeak. I lie still for a long time so the woman down the hall won't think I'm in here beating my meat. Women hate it when guys masturbate on their sheets (I learned about that sin from Sue Ann), so even as I am preoccupied by needing to sleep, my monkey — a childhood name — starts rising to spite me, demanding entertainment, all the while my heart scaring me to death by pounding so fast. I get up and tiptoe down the hall to the can and try to get it off over the toilet but nothing doing. I mean zip, limp. The bathroom is frilly and smells like powder.

Back I go on tiptoe, carefully slide into the cot and up he goes again, ready to rock and roll. It's not Sue Ann I want, it's more like Graciella, the sweet child part of her, and then my eyes close as though I am hypnotizing myself and my swollen part shrinks but, ha, stays swollen, waving in the breeze of somebody's laughter. Big lips swoop onto me and shit! I come all over this nice lady's sheets but I hurt and it was no fun at all. Creep back to the bathroom. Clean myself, wring the washcloth almost dry, unroll a wad of toilet paper, back to the spare room. Wipe, blot, sniff, lie down on the wet spot. The shivers start as I think about that big wet mouth.

Ashamed to face my hostess, I leave the next morning before breakfast. It's not like me to be rude, but I feel shitty, out of my head. I hitch up the mountain to Jerome, a "ghost town" full of expensive shops and tourists, but it's cooler than in the valley, there's a breeze up here, and I comb my hair in the museum restroom, hang out with old saddles and photos of mining dudes that look a lot like me and generally get a perspective on things. But the second night, camping under my jacket on a bench, the shivering starts again. The cold chills make me think somebody is pushing ice along my arms and chest, down my legs, into my head. A death wind quakes through my body. Yet I can't awaken fully; my eyes are glued shut. Something plays with my little monkey and the nightmare cranks up and I hear faraway laughter, feel that same breathiness as I get erect against my wishes — shit! — and come inside my jeans. My penis hurts like hell. This sex is no fun at all, and now I am a mess, moaning and lying on my back in the darkness, using all my will to push my eyes open to see a few stars raking the sky overhead and all I can think of is getting out of the park before someone ventures along and finds me in my shame. Those are the words that tackle me: *my shame*.

As it turns out, the last come was like a dry heave: lots of action but nothing delivered. An aching stays in my groin but at least I don't smell like a pervert. A gum-chewing waitress drives me as far as Clarkdale, on the outskirts of Cottonwood, and then I walk and trudge and finally catch a local bus and arrive home just after dark. Sue Ann is waiting at the screen door, leaning on the carpet sweeper. She's not surprised to see me.

"Welcome home, Romeo," she says. She never was a real warm person; she has a brown thumb that kills any growing thing. Me, I am prepared to throw myself into her arms and cut my hair, be Dudley Do-Right at long last. Except that I fall for her set-up.

"Romeo?" I ask. And she steps aside, reveals Graciella

bouncing one of my babies, the boy, on her hip. Poor Sue Ann is my first thought, although it ought to have been for my safety. Because after she opens the screen door, the next thing she does is swing the chunky end of the carpet sweeper like a croquet mallet right at my groin. It hits me where she's aimed it, I hear a gasp that might come from my own chest as I fly backwards, arching with the pain, arms milling, and fall down the steps. I end as a heap on the brick-coloured gravel. I try my jaw to see if it's dislocated and detect an ominous clicking.

Louise is standing behind me, huffing and snorting. "Far out!" I test the condition of my teeth and tongue by grimacing. No teeth fall out and my tongue still works. "She hit me," I announce to the world at large. Then Clarissa is standing over me but I hesitate to turn my head in her direction in case my neck is broken. There's sort of a whine working its way back into my voice, which is disheartening, reminding me of my younger self. I sound like I did when I slugged Matthew first and wanted Mum to think he hit me first because I was her favourite and the littlest.

Graciella steps aside, handing the baby to Sue Ann. She floats down the stairs to help me. "A spirit did it," she says in my ear. I hurt everywhere and feel spinny. I am half-prone on the ground, resting on an elbow like a dazed boxer.

"I never touched him," Sue Ann adds. The baby thinks I'm funny. Wide-eyed and drooling, he's pointing his finger at me. During the eleven days I was away, the babies got bigger, Sue Ann got thinner and nicer looking and Clarissa got a new job, driving a jeep and being a sunset tour guide in Sedona. "They like my beads and wisdom, you know?" is how she was modestly putting it to anybody and everybody. I don't find out what happened with the healing centre job, except maybe the honcho flipped out and went to Texas for alcohol rehab or maybe it was Clarissa who flipped out; sometimes it's hard to get the stories straight. Graciella beat me to Cottonwood by three days but was so good with the babies that Sue Ann invited her to stay on.

"Hey, come on, people," Clarissa says now, in her take-charge mode. "Louise, did you see Sue Ann hit Bobby?"

"A spirit did it," pronounces Louise, narrowing her eyes at me. "It was black with red around the outside. It left."

"It's true," says Graciella. "The child caused it." A fly is buzzing around my ears. I swat at it, look up to catch Louise staring at Graciella and Graciella is sending something from her eyes so that Louise steps back. Clarissa is saying, "You did what to Bobby?" asking Louise, who doesn't hear, she's got the fly on her now and it's Graciella into the totally weird. Sue Ann fades inside with the babies like she doesn't have a clue how charged the atmosphere is around us and Clarissa, having asked the big question, leaves to answer her phone. The fly has landed on Louise's skinny arm. She doesn't try to shake it off; she glares at it, malevolent as all hell. I get the shivers again and that and the fly is how I know she is a witch, she's jinxed me, this whole time has been Louise getting revenge. The goddess in my pocket burns my thigh. "Christ," I yelp and lean back, dig it out with trembling fingers, toss it. It lands at Louise's feet. She stoops to pick it up.

"No." Graciella makes a sudden move. "He must cleanse himself, bury it."

"I don't know nothing about spirits," Louise shouts. "I just made that part up." She takes off running. She's just a little kid.

I sit right where I am on the ground and fold my arms around my knees. There's a waft of breeze from the river. Duane sent a note with Graciella when he dumped her, signed "Yours in spirit." I think I've had enough with spirits.

Graciella spreads her skirt and eases down beside me. We just listen to the crickets. Then Graciella gestures towards the little stone goddess and instructs about sage cleanses and sacred fire and a root of something or other and how I'm supposed to bury the statue. I'm listening and not listening. Then the old lady, the one who likes my babies, wanders over and asks me how old I am. "Five," I say. "Me too," she chortles, like this is a great and true idea. She wants to join us on the ground and we watch her grappling with her brittle bones to get settled. She smooths her dress over her calves. You can hear the air conditioners rattling all through Cottonwood Trailer Park. You can hear pans banging and somebody tinkering with his car. You can hear TVs talking, the sound of applause.

Pee seeps out from under the old lady, who is looking around vacantly pleased. "Christ," I groan. Graciella shrugs. "It's life." The shivers run through me, head to toe, racing up and down my spine while I consider life. I figure I've done enough damage; it's time to call Matthew and go back home, taking Graciella and Sue Ann and my babies. The Fall FunFest should be on about now, and the whole town will be having a blast. I have this ideal image of us in Ruth and then I pass out or fall asleep, it's hard to tell which.

ROAD'S END

I WAS IN OCCAM'S CABIN with the VCR running when she knocked on the door. The screen was mostly hanging where my fist had bashed it deliberately, ripping the stapled edges from a frame that was in sad condition anyway. It was a way of making myself repair the sucker, which had needed repairing ever since my step-pop said he was quitting the resort business. When he told me, he rammed his foot into the same screen, and I thought later that this screen-attacking must be some male rite we were into. The slovenly hinges on all our doors and the rusted, sagging screen certainly represented for me all that was wrong with Sam Hill Road's End Resort and Boat Rental.

It was just after ten in the morning and the door was open when Jannette Giffin knocked. I knew her from the Marina Gallery and Zoo Café, where she was a new waitress and where I had my dry toast and hot chocolate with two added creams at eight a.m. most days. The Zoo was just on the other side of the bluff. A precarious, rock-embedded foot trail that I'd named Highpoint when I was a kid connected me to it.

She said, "Hello. Excuse me. Sorry. Sorry to disturb you."

I clicked off the movie, heaved myself off the davenport and invited her in. She refused. "I don't go into men's living quarters," she said after a pause. She stayed on the porch and sat awkwardly on the arm of an overstuffed chair. The porch too was rotten, in that sagging condition of all weathered old porches, and the chairs were past saving, lopsided from a missing foot or the seats sprung. I sighed and went out, letting what was left of the screen door bang. I said the usual "What brings you here, nice day, eh," as though I weren't depressed to my guts, as though Jannette Giffin routinely paid a call. She was not a pretty woman, she had a good-sized butt and a pocked face, and she was accident-prone, so the rumour went; she showed up at work scratched by tree limbs or her kid's toys or cats, or cut, burned or scalded from kitchen accidents at home. She had curly yellow hair, probably dyed; she belonged to a type of woman who always looked older than her years. But I hadn't thought much about her except that she remembered the two extra creams if Maggie or Dell forgot in the screech and bustle of breakfast at the Zoo.

It was the middle of a rain-soaked June, and the first sun we'd seen in weeks was muzzily poking through the layers of gloomy clouds that were beginning to feel permanent. The touch of warmer air renewed hope for a real summer. She turned to face the mountains across the lake. She said, "I hear your old man is giving you Road's End to run."

The End was a shanty cabin outfit with a few old outboards to rent. Ian and I didn't always get along, but he put up with my comings and goings because he needed me. I could fix things, the motors he wouldn't buy new, the clunker washer and dryer in the washhouse out back. He kept a clean set-up where it counted, in that once you climbed between the sheets you were all right; but he was not much for sweeping or decorating, and the loose-handled pots and pans on the open shelves were aluminum that nobody would be wanting to use any more because of the connection between aluminum and Alzheimer's. His customers were the good old boys out for a swamp-time, out from behind the lawnmowers and the sight of frilly kitchen curtains. Through my late teens I'd fantasized about making the End into a moneymaker, something yuppified and borderline first-class, yet keeping a genuine rustic quality. But when Ian left Occam's Cabin, what I considered home, to move to the new one up the mountain across the road, packing slabs of new-cured bacon and a case of whisky, it was like he took whatever initiative I ever had with him. Since, I had been lying around analys-ing movies, a sign I was in the pits. The characters, played by Matt Dillon and Nicolas Cage, seemed to do a lot of lying around between bouts of screwing, driving or steal-ing. In the lying-around department I was simpatico with these modern heroes. Also, watching all those highways go by reminded me of the generally sorry shape of the North American infrastructure, which plunged me deeper.

"You look like a man who needs help. I'm ambitious, I'm a good worker," said Jannette.

I had almost forgotten her, lost in thought about my own subversive infrastructure. "What do you mean?"

"Lord, you are something. I am offering here to help you get this shithole together."

"Oh." I was still behaving like somebody up to the ying-yang in muck until I thought of something to say. I asked her to leave her phone number.

She shook her head in disgust, wrote her number on her order pad and tore it off. She ignored my outstretched hand and put the paper on the chair cushion. "You need exercise," she said then, taking the steps two at a time. "At least get an extension cord, haul your damn TV outside for some fresh air."

I went in and checked the calendar pinned up over the phone table. The season openers, a bunch of rowdies from Calgary, were due in twelve days. They were booked into Grizzly, our biggest cabin and the one that slept seven, not counting the cots on the porch. I was in trouble. The sheets were in shreds due to age and the washer going berserk before biting the dust one afternoon last week; and in the loft there were nests of daddy longlegs, I thought they might be, and who knew what else. I paced the circles of the braid rug, then rewound the movie and headed over to the Zoo.

What they have at the Zoo Café are three parrots in two cages and some wild ducks, canvasbacks and mergansers, which hang around the water's edge; and in summer, prolific Canada geese and a lamb in a pen, a one-animal petting zoo. They have a few sad-looking lobsters in a tank, a short-haired ginger tom with a shredded ear and an arthritic black Lab. Marge and Sam, after whom Sam Hill Road was named, had big dreams. They heard the Germans were coming to build a world-class health resort for worn-out executives. Consequently, they sold a few up-lake parcels of land for a steep price and built the Zoo, Sam getting on the council to ensure zoning was approved. Next they added the Marina Gallery, with picture windows onto the scenery, where eventually they intended to put in a lakeside bar for all the hotshot execs cruising our lake in their high-powered rental tubs. Then the German deal fell through and Marge became a tyrant in the kitchen, scrimping on this and that, which dried up the local trade; so Sam went back to cooking, where his talents really lay, and now they've got steady, year-round business with reservations required for weekend dinners in the summer. These days Marge and Sam are torn between excitement and dismay, because it's rumoured the Japanese are planning a world-class ski resort, ski lifts mounting glaciers and a whole village to be constructed at the head of Pinenut Creek, whose name they'll change to Roaring Waters Creek or Black Bear Creek, something more imagistic for advertising purposes. The problem from Marge and Sam's point of view is that the road may not cut through to our side of the mountains.

Jannette was punching the order bell when I slipped in and sat at the counter. Her son, Jeremy, an overweight kid with yellow hair, almost white, really, was at a table on the deck outside the kitchen door. Sometimes the Korean prep cook would talk to him or occasionally Sam would hand him a fresh-made biscuit. Otherwise, the kid sat out there at a table of his own with an umbrella over it and drew pictures in his notebook. He drew with his tongue out and when he wasn't drawing he stared right through you with the coolest eyes I ever saw.

It was obvious Jannette wasn't going to pay me any attention until her lunch break. I don't know why I slumped on the stool lethargic as a creature hibernating when I could have been getting started at the End, maybe driving to Tucker to The Bay for some sheets. I nursed a coffee, picking at a plate of Sam's special home-cut fries and gravy, too weary to worry about cholesterol, until Jannette bent over and hissed in my ear, "Get out back. Lord."

She headed uphill towards the park, where there's a bench and a lookout spot. Down below Jeremy was plugging away at his art. She followed my gaze. "He's a good drawer," she said. "I bet he'll get a show in the gallery someday, he's that good. Dedicated. Ambitious."

She shot me a look.

"Right," I said, to be agreeable.

"You shouldn't have come here. Shift work or not, I don't want to lose my job. I was on a break when I come over to you."

I said, "I thought maybe I should strike while the iron is hot."

She considered whether I was being smart-ass and apparently gave me the benefit of the doubt, which is more than I might have done. She said, "Okay. I want a living wage. I want Jeremy to be able to stick around until school starts. I can't afford a babysitter and he don't know anybody yet." She frowned and added, "He's shy." She began a list on her fingers. "Living wage. Jeremy. Regular hours, no shift work. No social shit with the customers. I don't go for that. You and me never alone together."

She was so bizarre, the way she was enumerating her requests as though a normal person would consider them normal, that I laughed. I noticed her eyes, on the small side but alive with private fireworks, an engine behind them, not like women who have those big, up-front eyes: what you see at first glance is all you ever get.

Jannette said, "You don't understand."

I didn't and admitted it.

She ran her palms along her thighs and rolled up her sleeves and fluffed up her hair. Her actions weren't provocative so much as nervous, something on her mind. She was wearing the usual Zoo uniform, white blouse and tight black pants. On the undersides of her arms were ridges which I recognized as keloids, the result of skin not healing properly after a cut. Instead of knitting invisibly where it meets, the skin collides and forms an ugly hump. I had a ragged one myself on the inner part of my knee, from a chainsaw run amok.

Seeing my look, she yanked her sleeves down. "Nosy, aren't you," she said before I had a chance to explain. The woman was full of surprises. "That's from a car accident," she said. "I was nineteen and a half-ton truck hit us, a car full of kids. Anything else you want to know? I gotta get back. Usually I eat with Jeremy. I thought maybe you had a job to offer."

"Maybe I do," I said, busy calculating my savings from tree planting and salmon fishing that were tucked away in banks and credit unions from here to Vancouver, as well as what "living wage" might mean to a woman raising a kid.

She stood up, blocking the sun, casting me in shadow. She was waiting for an answer. I named a figure and she said, "That much?" and I said, "Yes," and she said, "Guaranteed?"

I almost said *lifetime*, the perfect flip remark to end our verbal volley. But Jannette was in earnest, something important seemed to be on the line for her, and I bit my tongue and gave her a simple yes.

In retrospect, it's easy to see that you don't necessarily pick people who are sensible for you or even, at times, sensible. Jannette possessed qualities I did not have. Like any regular guy I assumed that I had vision and initiative just because I was male. I was thirty-one, with a pretty good record of only a few winters on UIC behind me. While I liked some things other guys didn't — books and cooking — I could drink with the best and talk my way out of a brawl. I was a known hard worker. I had had my share of girlfriends and was considered a catch by some. I was lanky, topped six feet, and from what they all said, I was sweet. But until Jannette burst onto the scene, I hadn't faced how lackadaisical I was. That my fantasies for the End were only in my mind. That while I could fix almost anything when told, I couldn't grasp the whole picture; instead, what I got for trying was anxiety, and what I did about that was watch movies intently, preparing for my grown-up career as a Sunday morning movie reviewer for CBC radio. What

I had been busy doing when Jannette caught me hunched on the davenport, becoming paler by the hour, was mentally preparing for my real life, whenever it arrived.

Wearing jeans and a Bugle Boys sweatshirt, she arrived at the End after her shift that same afternoon. She pulled aside the ragged screen and shouted, "I don't suppose you have any Mr. Clean, a bucket that doesn't leak, a decent mop, sponges and a box of Brillo, eh?"

I didn't know why she was shouting, as I was sitting three feet from her. But with Jannette I soon learned that she was efficient and organized, and if she was accident-prone, it didn't show in her work; but I also learned there was no explaining some of her behaviour. That I just chalked up to eccentricity, a quality I respected.

She started on the bathroom in Grizzly, which demonstrated courage. Mostly groups of guys stayed in the cabin and it stank. I said they liked it that way because it did not remind them of home. She and I addressed the dirt question, sitting on the steps, her with a cigarette in her teeth and me admiring her ruggedness from the two-and-a-half-foot distance she made me keep. We talked about how clean the End should look. She was against bugs, fleas and spiders. I agreed. People did not drive in from the cities to be eaten; it left a bad impression on their skins and in their minds. She thought spick and span was the goal everywhere and I thought some dirt was okay, as long as it wasn't what Mum used to call "dirty dirt." We talked about what would qualify. The dirt talk lasted on and off for the first few days before we came to an agreement.

Clean dirt could have woodchips and dried leaves or pine needles in it and dirty dirt was the greasy kind.

Jannette came from Winnipeg, taking the long road round to wind up in Ruth. I don't know how she chose Ruth, but she had a stake in our town, buying the trailer from Billy Viola like she did, paying six thousand dollars cash, surprising him silly. He moved his drums and mattress out of there in record time when she flashed the money at him. She went banging on his door one Sunday noon, and he was still sleeping, he'd had a gig in an up-lake settlement called the Neon Bar the night before. He answered the door shorts only and no doubt foul of breath and tongue, I knew, because Billy Viola was an old buddy of mine and hated being awake in the daytime. But she flashed the money at him like she was born to it, he said, pulled it out of her jeans pocket in this bundle and just rolled it past his greed-stricken eyes. Told him she wanted the place left clean. He was out of there on Monday in enough time for a woman to come in, and on Tuesday Jannette and Jeremy moved in. Jeremy, I gathered, was eight.

The next morning at our coffee break I asked Jannette if I could take him, Jeremy, in the van to Tucker to buy the sheets, and she said no. We were standing on the dock watching some Canada geese feed, Jannette and I each with coffee mugs in our hands, the coffee Kona roast, beans so expensive I used the hand-grinder, Jeremy beside us dressed in cords and matching olive sweater, like a kid going off to school rather than one embarked on a carefree summer.

Apparently Jeremy hadn't liked being in a new school so close to end of term, so she had withdrawn him. He didn't do anything I might have done at his age, like chase the geese or try to feed them. He was standing with us because we had called him down from the porch of Grizzly, where Jannette had parked him while she vacuumed the cobwebs from the log walls.

"Why not?" I said. "He's just going to hang around here all day watching you."

She scalded me with a look that meant none of your beeswax, bub. She said, "I am going to be watching him, because I am a fit mother and know better than to let my child go off in a vehicle with a stranger."

Jannette had this thing about being a "fit mother." The story that she told me was melodramatic for my taste. She seemed to be on the run from Jeremy's father, who wanted custody of him after the divorce became final. She seemed to think that the father might have damning evidence against her that a judge would believe, but that she wouldn't talk about.

"Somebody's got to get the sheets," I said. "I forgot to order them from Sears in time."

"You would," she said. "Eh, Jeremy. He would, eh?"

Jeremy turned and sighed. He was an old-man child, lethargic and too plump in the butt. To get in shape I figured he ought to run behind the van like Mickey's golden retriever ran behind the town's backhoe. Every grade school has a few kids like Jeremy. The flabby type with soft hands, teachers' pets.

I said, "Doesn't he have any suitable clothes? For a kid his age? Summer?"

She glared at me again and I let her. "We left in a hurry."

"Fine, have it your way. But in Tucker they have a Bay with everything in it, three storeys." I watched the geese intently. They were skirting the dock, breaking into sets, one group reconnoitring, the others hanging back. There must have been forty of them. I was giving her a chance to think.

"Okay," she said. "We'll go. But it'll mean making up the time, me working late when we get back, all the lights on, and Jeremy in my possession every second and you no-where to be seen. You got it?"

I did and we piled into the van, an Econoline with no windows in the back, the three of us in the front seat.

"This will not do," Jannette said. She flung open the door. "Out, Jeremy."

I barely had time to turn off the engine before she lit in. "What do you think it would look like, us driving through town like some kind of family? Do you think I'm out of my mind? Are you working for him? Is that it? Is that why you're paying me so much, this is some kind of trap? Oh, my Lord. Jeremy! Jeremy!"

She had the kid by the sleeve, heading to her beat-up Tempo, fender falling off, one door handle missing in the back. "I knew it," she was muttering. "This was too good to be true, this job, you, everything! Oh, my Lord!"

She threw herself behind the wheel and Jeremy dived

for the back seat. I ran over, waving my arms, but she was already backing out, skidding on gravel, creating billowing dust. The car fishtailed up the steep section of Sam Hill Road. Jeremy, in the back window, stuck his tongue out.

We'd lost a day and a half of work before she showed up again, but I wasn't "house proud" yet and not particularly concerned about what the cowboys due in day after tomorrow would think. Probably they wouldn't notice the improvements in the general hygiene of Grizzly; probably all they would care about was the big Starcraft being ship-shape. I had bought one of those safety rigs; the designated driver wears the key chain connected to his belt, so if the key is pulled out of the ignition, the motor stops. This was in the event they all got pissed and fell overboard. Last year a fellow was out in the lake freezing his balls while our Lund circled him full throttle until sputtering out of gas. That there wasn't much gas in it in the first place was a hundred per cent Ian and that fellow's good luck.

Jannette's car door hardly made a sound and her step, as she came down the slope towards where I was working, wasn't authoritative. I was polishing the van, not knowing why; of all the things that needed doing, polishing the van would be near the last on any sensible person's list, if it made the list at all, but there I was, a chamois and Turtle Wax in hand.

"This place needs some flowers, landscaping, that shit," she said from behind me. I sensed she was waiting for me to turn around. My heart began knocking in my

chest as though I knew intuitively I was going to be dis-
tressed by what I saw. I took my time, but when I glanced
her way, the condition of her face shocked me, and I went
back to polishing the crap out of a dent made by a gal at
the hardware store in Tucker when she was late to a district chamber meeting.

Jannette's forehead was scraped raw, scratches filled
with dried blood that I could see through the hair she tried
to pull down over it, as though she'd been clawed. Her
eyelids were swollen; there was a Band-Aid partially hiding an evil-looking gouge in her cheek. Hers was the kind
of face that without extra help looked like it was having
a hard life. But now it was gruesome. My mind raced
through possibilities: she was riding a bicycle downhill and
lost control. She had stopped suddenly in that stupid car
of hers, and not wearing a seat belt had bashed her face on
the dash or the windshield. A boyfriend had beat her up.
This last was what I feared the most.

She said, "I was carrying fertilizer, you know one of
those big bags, for our garden. The one me and Jeremy are
going to start, isn't that right, Jeremy, eh? Aren't we? And
I tripped on a skateboard, not Jeremy's, he don't go in for
skating, although maybe he ought to, oh, I don't know,
some lousy neighbour kid left it on our walk, eh, and I
tripped, crash bang, smack onto the sidewalk like a ton of
bricks. And that's the story, folks." She giggled and said,
"They used to say that on the news. I think that's where I
heard it, 'the story, folks,' tune in tomorrow, same time,
same station."

It was not like Jannette to be chatty, and she was not a giggler. I carefully draped the chamois on the door handle and leaned back against the van, arms folded, and considered her. I noticed she had slathered some kind of clear lotion, probably antiseptic, on her forehead wounds. She could not look me in the eye. Giggles emitted from her as though she was drunk on champagne.

Jeremy had slunk off to a nearby picnic table. He sat at a safe distance, hands over his ears, and watched us.

"What happened?" I asked. The question took all my courage, because the change in her frightened me. I was thinking that maybe I didn't believe the stories about her being accident-prone, but I didn't know what else to think. And I was confused about the boyfriend I had so obligingly invented for her. Ruth wasn't an especially big town, and if she had a boyfriend, especially a bastard, likely I would have heard his name.

Jannette shut up. There was a hint of breeze from the south, and clouds were gathering over the mountains to the east. The lake began to move and rock against the shore. Off in the distance you could hear a loon, unusual in our neck of the woods, and no answer, although they tended to travel in pairs. A logging truck rumbled up on the highway and then the silence was back again, becoming more awkward between us, until I broke. I called over to Jeremy to come on back, aware of Jannette tense and mute beside me, wondering what I was up to. Simply, I was getting us both out of this mess. When Jeremy refused, stayed at the table, I called my idea to him, elaborating on it and repeating myself, although it wasn't in my nature to raise my voice. Basically I said I was going into Tucker, and that I could get him some summer clothes, some neat gear. What was his favourite colour?

Reluctantly he told me, blue. Jannette's gratitude was palpable. My heart welled, as though I were God granting grace to a sinner. In the next moment my pride sickened me and I felt angry, as if my feelings were her fault. I reached for the chamois. It slid to the ground and Jannette scurried to snatch it up and hand it back. I couldn't stand that either, how eager she was to please me. I dived into the van, slammed the door, spewed gravel and dirt as I tore up to the highway.

After passing through town going too fast, I realized I didn't have my wallet with me. I would have to turn around. But then almost back to the turn-off to the End, I realized I didn't want to see Jannette. I was focusing on her love life. If she was so stupid as to let a man hit her, maybe a guy she'd picked up in a bar, for all I knew, it was none of my business. Lots of women were into abuse, everybody knew it. Questions nagged me, however — I would have heard; and I'd been in local bars and beer parlours often enough myself and had never seen her or overheard any talk about her. And I knew what a beat-up woman looked like, Ruth had its share. So far as I knew, Jannette's abrasions didn't fit the category; there was no basic black eye or dislocated jaw, no generalized swelling. Her eyelids were puffy and reddened like she'd been crying for hours, I knew that condition well from when I was a kid; it was how my mum frequently looked. I U-turned again, roared back into town and took out cash from the Credit Union. "Some serious grocery shopping," I said self-consciously to Marianne behind the wicket, as though anybody cared what I was doing or what I wanted the money for.

Case-lot sales were in the fall. Whenever I wasn't working out of town, I avidly collected the store flyers from the mailbox and perused them, circling in marking pen the best buys and then checking those prices with the wholesalers where Ian bought. Sometimes the prices were better at the retail stores, incentive buys to get customers in. I would outsmart them and buy just the specials, cases of toilet paper or paper towels or even canned beans one year. (It had been my idea to stock the cabins with pork and beans and a can opener, as a gesture of welcome for road-weary travellers, and it worked. Guys liked it.) Occam's Cabin had a good-sized root cellar, and although I didn't go in for canning, Ian let me bring in the supplies. We kept stocks of paper goods and cleaning supplies (underused) and for our own use, ketchup (Ian insisted), Worcestershire sauce, tuna, canned soups and fold-lock-top sandwich bags, my personal favourite. If I was depressed I sometimes had enough sense to take myself down to the root cellar and sit a while. The temperature was cool and it smelled of packed earth with hints of mildew and spider web, and it was peaceful. The cardboard boxes of twelve of this or twenty-four of that were reassuring. Some were lightweight, you could toss a bulky paper-towel box into the air, while others were dense and heavy, like the sock-eye salmon or mayonnaise. I would touch them, try lifting them, pull up the flaps and peer inside, and after a while cheer up.

In Tucker, I spent my cash down to the nickel and regretted not having my credit cards because I had come across some prize finds. The back of the van was loaded with potting soil mixes and fertilizers and clay pots and cedar boxes, on sale at the Tucker nursery. I bought various sizes because Jannette was right; we should start some landscaping. It was almost too late — it was June 29 by then — and the bedding plants looked picked over but I chose the least withered, the largest and leafiest. I didn't believe her fertilizer story or that she intended to do a garden at her place, but a garden was a good idea for the End. If I wanted to change the nature of my clientele, maybe get more family trade or couples, we would have to do more than clean the units, we would have to spruce up the whole place, make it appeal to somebody besides old guys into fishing, destruction and beer.

Jannette helped me pack my other bargains, facial tissues and Sani-Flush from Canadian Tire, into the cellar of Occam. As she came down the old wooden stairs into the root cellar, she gave an excited gasp. Obviously she felt the same about stockpiling as I did, though the boxes of what was left had been torn open impatiently by Ian, and my neat piles and categories were messed up. The look in her eyes was euphoric, even if the rest of her face made me wince.

Her looking like that, I couldn't hang around. I went to the hotel bar to hunt up some of the guys, telling myself I was celebrating the turning point of Road's End. I got back late with a head the size of P.E.I. The porch light was on, a weak yellowed bulb encrusted with fly crap. In the light I saw that Jannette had planted lobelia, pansies and geraniums in one of the new cedar boxes and left it on the railing. I managed to knock it over while peering closer, sniffing the leaves, who knew what I was doing, and then, to compensate, I planted another bunch and then another so that maybe she wouldn't notice, but of course she did, spotted it first thing in the morning, the streaks of unswept loamy potting soil on the porch and my clumsy, undisciplined efforts. We looked at each other through the wrecked screen, her forehead less raw but her cheek more bruised than yesterday and me with a pounding head and feeling vaguely bruised myself. She didn't say a word about the damage, nor did I.

Over the next few nights, I fell into a familiar self-hate litany as much a part of me as breath. Typically, like this morning, having slept in my damn clothes — fell asleep watching TV, clicked it off sometime in the night — I came to, groggy and sick, to face my overactive brain sending me negative messages. Ran with it, through the long, long letter of farewell, right to suicide — this time jumping into the lake from Highpoint, splitting my gourd on a submerged boulder — and then heaved myself from the davenport and made coffee. The chain of internal events started near bedtime with the customary *Good God, you two drive me crazy. Go on, go away, leave me alone, can't you ever leave me alone?* From there the grey matter clicked into random mode, whirring like the insane disk drive on the old Apple II. I drank a carton of milk, for the calming effects of the tryptophan. Made the mistake of opening the freezer and noticing the half-eaten Sara Lee cake. Back in the living room, realized the chocolate in the cake was undoing the tryptophan. Decided what I needed was alcohol to settle down.

Glass in hand, thought of writing Bobby, in Arizona. Hey, bro, how goes it? But then a quick shower seemed like a good idea. Out of the shower, felt buoyed and on the right track. Lay on the davenport to channel-surf a while. Just as relaxation was settling in, the nerves in my upper arms ignited and I was pricked with guilt: I should have bought that sink advertised in the *Ruth Gazetteer*, as Jannette had told me to do. All the cabins needed new sinks. The more I dwelled on it, the more I was sure I had missed the deal of a lifetime. I poured another vodka neat, stared out into the night, told myself there were other sinks in the world. After a bit, my behaviour disgusted me, the constant self-undermining, the resultant refuge I took in drink. There was no way I could write Bobby, I was too depressed.

So then I headed back to the davenport, turned up the TV. These internal electrical events, the random firing of synapses, these disturbances the family was prone to attacked worse when the moon was full, so Mum always said. As for her, I guess she was the expert. As a boy I'd seen her curled up, unspeaking, for whole days on the very same davenport. I thought she was sad because of their fighting, her and our step-pop. Their battles were nerve-wrackingly silent, like being surrounded by bats near-missing in an attic. And then when I was twelve years old and Bobby eight, she left. Just took off. She left me and Bobby in the care of Ian, a man who had never indicated liking us boys very much. We woke up one morning to Ian stomping around the place, calling her an imbecilic bitch. Bobby sneaked into my bed, skinny body trembling, hid under the covers, his ear to my chest. We listened to Ian kicking trash cans behind the cabin.

Now, a whole different scene was taking place at the End, this one between Jannette and Jeremy. I was peering through binoculars, spying on them, elbows on the freezer off the kitchen, coffee cooling in the mug beside me. As the kettle was boiling, I'd heard Jannette give an exasperated shout. I poured the boiling water through the cone, waited for another sound. Nothing. Budding heroic characteristics in me considered going out to see what was up, but I came to my senses. The fact of Jannette's moody, unpredictable nature gave me pause; people could get hurt. Besides, I felt like run-over dog poop.

I shifted to get a better view. Jeremy was leading his mother by the hand towards the new picnic table in front of the cabin called Badger. She was placid with him, sat as he directed and waited while he waddled back to the porch to bring down her cigarettes and a lighter from the purse hanging by its strap over the railing. She tended to keep her purse with her all the time, in sight of one or both of them, so she could make a fast getaway, I supposed; it didn't make any other sense to me. She had an aura of being pursued; it was partly why she was intriguing. The kid was back, sitting beside her, his shoulder touching her arm. She lit up. They didn't seem to be saying much, they seldom did, but I had to acknowledge that between them there was a communication that made me queasy. Her dragging the kid to work every day didn't seem natural. I mean, it was summer, he should be playing with friends, goofing around, sneaking through woods, the kind of things kids did in Ruth. Like what Bobby and I had done, normal kid stuff. And it wasn't that Jeremy was a pest. Just the opposite: he was so prissy I wanted to belt him one to get the testosterone going. The relationship between him and his mother was perplexing, especially since the kid was charmless as a lump of unrisen dough. And I found myself thinking, What the hell, Bobby had been *cute*, really appealing. There was no explaining some things. I hated how my mind was like a hungry pig, rooting in the mud of the past as though a scrap could be found in that mire.

The sun had come out from behind the trees. It seemed possible that my bent mind had created the whole uproar. I slugged back the coffee, rinsed my cup, put it in the rack. I threw water on my face, smoothed my hair down. Then I went outside, letting the back door bang so they'd know I was coming. The scene that met me was tranquil: Jeremy at the picnic table, scribbling on his endless drawing pad, Jannette smoking on the porch steps.

In the angle of light Jannette's yellow hair looked more kinked than curled. I could see the line around her head where the curlers had started. I imagined her giving herself a permanent in the sink, using pink and blue plastic rollers, as my mum had done, winding the strands into a square of paper (I could hear the click of the curler snapping), pouring nose-burning chemicals over the back of her head in the name of *beauty*.

Beauty was an odd idea to be associated with Jannette; it was the last sort of thing anybody'd say about her. As I ambled over, she blew out a stream of smoke. Closer, I noticed that she smelled of smoke, and added to it was a layer of enamel paint fumes from a project she thought was stupid. I'd made the mistake of asking her opinion about the colour for the floor paint in the cabins, and she'd made her point, that she was totally against paint on floors. It showed dust, it chipped. She'd called me a spoiled brat. "This place was handed to you on a fucking platter. At least you could do *vinyl*." Vinyl, she figured, would appeal to yuppies. She got into one of her loud states and yelled, "They got vinyl looks like real wood, and yuppies are into that sort of crap!" Obviously she was somebody who cared passionately about what happened to floors. I admired this attitude, actually; it tended to make up for her secretiveness, her defensiveness, the whole mysterious package.

I casually asked her how it was going.

"Who wants to know and why?" She exhaled and looked down at her bitten nails.

I took a breath and plunged on. "I just happened to

notice you were — well, it was my impression that you were, uh, freaked out" — I was at my most articulate around her — "and I happened to be taking a breather from, uh, doing the books, you know, stretching the old arms, checking the weather, saw you and Jeremy and whatnot."

She stood up, with the manner of someone rising to a challenge. On the second step, she still only came to forehead level with me. "You think it's not normal for a perfectly normal kid to want to make his mum to feel better when she goofed? You think that's worth a trip into the open air, eh?"

I ducked to one side. I missed most of what she was saying; my attention was on how she made pronouncements without eye contact.

"What are you doing." It wasn't put as a question.

"I want you to look at me," I said, my heart taking a dive as soon as the words tumbled from my mouth. "It's just that — just that you don't look at the person you're talking to. I noticed it, eh."

She stepped past me, crushed her cigarette in the dirt, pocketed the butt, all her movements quick and spare. She stood with her shoulders squared and her hands tucked into the back pockets of her jeans. Because her back was to the lake, the sun was bright behind her and her features were in shadow. "I don't think you know nothing about kids and their mums and you had better not stick your nose where it's not wanted, that's what I think. I left a goddamned brand-new paintbrush in the cabin, Mr. Nosy. In the bedroom. Where it's trapped by a marine blue, just-painted floor that will be a dust catcher, but don't pay no attention to my opinion on the matter."

Jeremy was watching her. I couldn't tell his expression, I was too busy thinking, A *paintbrush*. Her tail was in a knot over a *paintbrush*. "Hey, gosh, don't worry about it," I said. "Please." I fumbled for my handkerchief and dabbed my forehead. "I mean," I said, thinking fast as she turned away, "I've got the mixings for a super crab-and-avocado sandwich — salad, too, what do you think? About coming up to the house for lunch?" She frowned. "With Jeremy, of course," I threw in.

She squinted in my direction. "You're not P O'd?"

"Heck, no," I said eloquently. "So, how about lunch?"

"If you want." Shrugging. "Outside. On the porch."

I was feeling fifteen again. "Great, sure. Noonish?"

Her mouth twitched. "Yeah, sure, *noonish*."

Which meant I had to drive into town to get the ingredients for this fantasy lunch, the canned crab and a couple of avocados. I drove along hoping the avocados I'd seen at the SuperValu the other day weren't overripe. I picked up a package of hot dogs for the kid — kids liked hot dogs, Bobby and I used to gnaw on them cold from the fridge. I chose some homestyle white bread from the bakery. She'd like that, I thought, assessing her as a white-bread eater. I stopped by the Sears catalogue store to pick up the sheets and throw rugs that came in yesterday. I was feeling virtuous as all hell. At the hardware I bought a paintbrush, dropped by the drugstore for a red bow.

"Lucky Deirdre," Corrina said, ringing up the bow.

Because we — Deirdre, Corrina and I — had all gone through school together, I supposed it was natural Corrina would make assumptions; Deirdre and I had been a couple on and off for years. Thinking of Deirdre, how great she was in the sack, colour rose up the back of my neck. Corrina smirked as she handed me the change. "Oh, I heard something. Some guy in here asking Mike — you know the new pharmacist? — about Jannette Giffin you got out there? And Mike, of course, didn't know nothing, but still.... Thin guy, leather jacket. Monster camera." She opened her eyes exaggeratedly wide and sealed her lips. The conspiracy mania of some women made me nuts. Then she winked as she accepted money for a lottery ticket from an eavesdropping old-timer.

Alcohol through the night and a day-old donut for breakfast were working their perverse magic; I knew if I tried to speak, even a simple thanks or goodbye, the words would choke me. I left the air-conditioned store, hit the street in bright sunshine. Despite the temperature, I suddenly couldn't stand this day, the jarring angles events were taking. Back in the Econoline, my mood on the downswing, I got to thinking that Jannette would not take well to the bow on the paintbrush. She would figure I was being patronizing or doing her some big favour. Same for the paintbrush itself. I tossed both bags into the back, feeling really, really aimlessly annoyed.

Where I went wrong at lunch was asking her about Winnipeg. It seemed a harmless enough conversational gambit but that's because I wasn't functioning optimally. I was fussing with the raspberry vinaigrette, adjusting the olive oil, busily whisking when Kraft in a damn bottle would have done. She froze at my question, the kid went into a blinking spasm watching her, and then I put my foot right in it, saying, "I thought it was, uh, you know, just a *life*."

She rose from the chair — I'd brought out the best ones, from the dining room, ratty, godforsaken things, seats in tattered strips of brocade — and said, "Don't we wish, eh, Jeremy," and clumped off. There went the radicchio and butter lettuce I'd spent all that money on, wasted. God in heaven, this woman was not Deirdre, not by a long shot.

By the afternoon, I was out bobbing not far from shore in my fifty-horse Lund. I had cashed in this day totally, considered it a wipe-out. I was enjoying caressing the two remaining cans of beer from the six-pack I brought with me, but I was also obsessing, reviewing the ridiculous lunch: I should have used the straw place mats with the grease spots instead of the nice tablecloth; a woman like her wouldn't know the difference. And I certainly had intended to pass on Corrina's news about the fellow asking about her, if only she hadn't buggered off so peremptorily. I was a ziphead to consider being attracted to someone like Jannette — by that time, I had faced the fact that I was toying with being attracted — much less to Jannette herself, a woman whose past life, for Christ's sake, was hunting her down. Was *bothering* to hunt her down. Her and that goddamn clump of a kid. That last fact pissed me off. I swigged from a mickey of rye. If I wanted to get shit-faced fast, the combination of beer and rye was a winner.

An osprey made a flirting swoop over the water. I pondered osprey family life, their big nests proudly visible. The Beatles song "All You Need Is Love" popped into my consciousness; the words introduced a maudlin note to the day. I began to sing, in a voice Mum once commented wasn't in tune with anything. Okay, it was bad for her back then — no electricity at Road's End except what Ian could coax from the noisy generator, no reliable phone service. She was destitute — "Yes, she was, yes she was, that's the word," I said to seagulls flapping by — desperate and made destitute by the change from town, where she could at least eat out once in a while, see a play, go to a tea. She didn't drive. God in heaven, I realized, what the hell kind of life. Toronto, now there was a real place. We'd received a postcard once.

But poor bro, I thought. Poor little guy.

I flicked my hair out of my face and noticed Jannette's damn kid on the dock, watching. Everywhere I went these days, there was that damn kid watching. I got to thinking: He'd never been out on Judith Lake, and for all I knew he'd never been in a boat. Jannette wouldn't let him. Here it was summer and he was wearing jeans (at least he wasn't still in those horrible cords). He couldn't wear shorts, she'd told me, because he was allergic to bugs, mosquitoes, anything with wings. She had him covered head to toe in repellent — the idea that he needed more repellent than he came by naturally made me snort — so he wouldn't have to have antihistamine shots. What a wuss that kid was.

Something took me over. I turned the boat towards the dock, revved it up. I wanted to see if he'd chicken and run off. Spray flying, I made right for him, had him targeted in the point of the bow. Kid had balls. I had to cut the engine and surf in, and he didn't recoil, either, when a curl of water dumped on him. "Boat ride, laddie?" I called, catching hold of the rope affixed to the dock. "Come on aboard." I had a grin like the wolf in *The Three Little Pigs*, I could feel it.

He returned a look like he had me totally cased. He said, "Can't. Mum won't let you take me. Wouldn't be good publicity."

Christ, this little twit had an obnoxious manner. But he did snag my curiosity when he mentioned the publicity bit.

He dropped a corner of his mouth. "Duh. For the court case coming up. The guy with the camera. Over there." He pointed to a scrawny stand of ponderosa pines behind an outcropping of basalt. I fiddled with my glasses, bringing them up my nose, down again, making sure I was seeing what I thought. A man was half-hidden, with a monster lens on his camera, just as Corrina had described. I was devastated. The fellow, seeing us looking at him, stepped forward, snapped Jeremy and me together. He waved. He had some nerve to wave.

I couldn't believe, could not get it through my skull that Jannette's past life was making such a play for her — or rather, for *him*, for Jeremy. That a father would pay bucks to hire a detective to do whatever it took in order to get this particular kid back, the ugliest, dumbest kid in the world. "Get in," I said to Jeremy, and I grabbed the cuff of his jeans, held on.

Surprisingly he did as he was told and climbed into the boat, using all fours. When he was in, I made a big fuss about putting a life jacket on him. I smiled wildly at the camera, chuckled, loud enough for the photographer to hear: "Atta boy, there you go, another great day on the lake, eh?" I shoved us off. And then we were crashing across the water, the hull bumping over the swells. I took him fast. I didn't know what I was doing.

We got as far as the east side of Judith Island, away from prying eyes, and I circled and zigzagged over our wake and enjoyed watching his butt go bang, bang on the seat. I watched him turn green, and I had never felt so satisfyingly mean in my life. While I was gloating, up came his gobbled hot dog and half his mum's sandwich — I remember her giving half to him automatically — and in a panic, I killed the motor. He'd missed getting it over the side, messed one leg of his jeans. He looked awful, hunched in on himself, the orange life jacket up around his chin, foul spit dribbling from his mouth onto the jacket. For a second he looked as pathetic as Bobby waiting for me to heat up canned soup for dinner. "Christ," I said, feeling a little green myself, "are you all right?"

"Yeah, man." He wiped his mouth and rubbed his hands on the clean places on his jeans. He took off the life jacket and flung it in my direction, staring at me the whole time with an unpleasant intensity that made him seem older than eight. I tried to imagine what his father looked like: a big man, heavyset, ponderous, a man you didn't want to get on the wrong side of. I knew he owned a used-car lot, that he smoked cigars. His name was Warner. I tucked the life jacket in the well behind me, tossed the kid a rag that was fairly clean. "Miss your dad?" I asked.

"I was in a foster home once. They were cool. I miss *them*," he said.

I didn't know what to think and made a pretence of studying the clouds bunching overhead. "Ruth's an okay place," I offered. "My brother and I had some decent times."

"My dad was in the army," he shot back. "My dad has lots of friends, loads of dough. I want you to land this craft, mister. I ain't been on an island. Land this craft now, mister. That's an order."

The imperious little s.o.b. was pretty impressive with the movie lingo. "Sure," I said. "I mean, yes, *sir*."

He took off his shoes and socks and yanked up his jeans; and before I thought to warn him, he scrambled over the side with more agility than I suspected he had. He let loose a shocked yell — the water was damn cold — and thrashed about. The boat, drifting with the wind, nearly knocked him in the head before he managed to get himself upright and on the move. He refused my help and waded ashore like an army of one claiming the land for the Right and the True. (Bobby had come up with that one on his own; playing with blocks of wood and building kingdoms in our room, we became the emissaries for the Right and the True.) I admired this stupid kid, this kid with the uptown name, *Jeremy*, because he didn't let on that the rocks beneath the water were killing his tender feet.

In one barbaric moment, I understood the impulse of hit-and-run drivers. I thought of leaving him. It would be so easy: put the motor in reverse, back out of the tiny Judith Island Bay, go. At about the time my hand on the throttle was twitching, he turned and glared, as if reading my mind. Then, still eyeing me, he proceeded to lie on his back in the water at the shore, leaving only his face and belly and toes visible. God in heaven. He bolted up and yelled, "Come and get me, wimp turkey!" Then lay back, waited. Christ.

He stank of barf and weighed a ton. He kept his eyes closed as I slogged him through the cold water back to the boat, wrecking my sandals, hurting my back because of the precarious balancing act that was necessary to deal with his bulk, the stones underfoot, because of my own drunkenness and subsequent tension. The kid knew I wouldn't dare drop him. I could have bawled with envy.

Twenty minutes later, I solicitously helped him onto the dock, tied the boat out of the wind and scrabbled up the rocks to Highpoint Trail. I was heading for the Zoo Café and a bucket of their lead-belly coffee to sober me up. And food, lots of it. Midway, I wrapped my arms around a deeply cold boulder and wept. Glimpses of my chaotic behaviour began to filter through. How could I have behaved like such a jerk, waved at the camera, nabbed the kid? Everything Jannette didn't need, I had done: gone public, made like there was a relationship between me and the kid, and therefore, I supposed, a relationship with her, everything she had been so careful to avoid.

I pissed out a gallon of beer, watched my stream arc into space and splatter the scree. I remembered the morning's thoughts: head smashing on a boulder below waterline. Right. As though Jannette would let me get away with such a simple ending.

I hid at a back table, jumpy every time the door opened, suicidally eating plates of fries with gravy and battered chicken wings with blue-cheese dressing. I waited until six-thirty, way past the time Jannette was supposed to call it a day, then I set out for home. I needed sleep, I needed to get my excuses together.

Trotting along a sharp curve in the road, I spotted her ratched Tempo heading in my direction. My first thought was to dive into roadside bramble, but I was too near the driveway of a palatial house with a couple of supercharged searchlights. She was driving slow, as if she was on the lookout. Then she saw me, pulled a U-ey. I was in such a state of discombobulation, I could practically hear the childish, whiny excuses rising from my cowardly gut. I took a deep, preparatory breath as the car door slammed, and she came trundling around the front. She left the headlights on.

"Have you got a minute?" Her request was so formal that a movie addict's thought leapt to the forefront of my brain: She had a knife, she was planning to slide it between my ribs for my transgression. I sidled away, but she followed, gesticulating, speaking rapidly. She said, "Someone, uh, dropped by and told me there's a guy in town, a detective. Warner, the bastard, was serious, he's sent somebody. He *hired* somebody. He's out to get my baby. He's out to get my boy. Please, Matthew, you're my friend," she said, wringing her hands — no knife, I thought — not looking at me but using my name, making my ears throb with the sound of it in her throat. "Watch out for this guy, eh? He's taking evidence, anything he can get his hands on, like that I'm alienating Jeremy from his dad, that I'm no good." She sucked air through her teeth. "It's not true. Whatever you hear about me, it's not true. Look at him. A happy, normal boy, eh?"

I wasn't sure I'd heard correctly. We both turned to glance at the car. Jeremy had opened the passenger door and sat half in, half out, his legs and Prince Valiant hair visible in the light. I didn't like Jannette behaving in this manner: humble. Beseeching. It made me nauseated. I wanted to know why the hell she wasn't scratching my eyes out, why I wasn't deep-down *afraid*.

Jeremy hadn't told.

My mum's postcard from Toronto floated into my consciousness so clearly it was like holding it in my hand. On the back of the glittering city at night, Mum had written: "Working at Eaton's, buying season tickets to everything at the O'Keefe Centre." She wrote that she was born to be an audience and that she'd never been happier. She wished her "sweet boys" the best.

A car passed. On its tail, a truck honked in greeting, somebody from up the lake. It took effort to vault myself into the present. I blinked and looked at the kid. The kid looked back.

Nothing.

I heard myself muttering a reassuring speech to Jannette. About trust, about sticking together.

She sighed. "Okay, thanks a million." Her smile was so broad I caught the gleam of a silver-capped molar. She danced backwards towards the Tempo and, still beaming at me, reached out her hand for Jeremy. And he, the conniving little grinning bastard, slipped out of the car and took it.

Energy is matter and matter is energy; and the workings of mind, consciousness and body are one and the same.

Right. I took a breath at that line, pulled my shades down to study the bright light of August darting off the surface of the lake and ploughed on. We all had the potential to learn true awareness. All we needed to do was pay attention to our God-given intuition, which was the bridge that allowed what we perceived to be conflicting thoughts, or energies, to meet and bring us to unity.

That was my take on what the writer was saying. I was on the porch at Occam reading a slender volume by a practical mystic (that's what it said on the cover) named Joshua Harvey. I was feeling I could use a little intuition in my life. I was trying to get my head to a clear space before I went to Ian's place up the mountain, having received a phone call from a buddy in Tucker. My buddy works at the Bank of Montreal, and he came across a closed account for Road's End — he wouldn't say how much had been in it — an account closed a week or so before Ian gave the End to me, along with its puny local bank account. Ian hadn't mentioned any other money.

I liked the feel of the book as I held it in both hands. It had been printed by somebody who knew typeface and paper quality. I had always been identified as having academic potential, although in my experience having potential was a terrible thing; it was like being locked into a state forever unrealized. Off in the distance I could hear a boat trolling, some hopeful fool, probably a guest at the resort, who didn't know that fishing this time of year was a drag. I stirred, crinkled my beer can and threw it over the railing, then groaned aloud. Jannette would give me hell.

Ian had moved deep into the woods, across the highway and up a skidder's trail. The cabin itself was situated in a depression, surrounded by red cedar and hemlock that blocked the view of the lake. When I asked him about it, he said he didn't care to see the lake again, he'd seen enough of it to last a lifetime.

As I trudged past what looked like a newly dug parking area, junk began appearing: machine parts, busted wooden boxes, wood scraps and bursting garbage bags, tarps, newspapers and a scattering of candy-bar wrappers, mostly Snickers from the look of it. I think Ian felt most like a real man amidst trash; I think it was a macho thing for him, although he wasn't the type that comes to mind when you hear the term "macho." Basically he was bones and sinew, with grey stubble on his tight jowls — getting him to shave had been one of the banes of my mother's relatively short marriage to him — and even seeing him from a distance, I could tell that his hair was overgrown and askew. He had on a pair of jeans shredded at the knees — his shreds were genuine, from years of stubborn wear — and on his feet were the same scuffed-up Birkenstock sandals that he'd always worn.

His laconic Southern greeting was a heavy-handed affectation meant to be seen through. Originally from the States, from an uptown East Coast family, he had a master's degree in something intellectual and useless, like philosophy. My mother, who had only a high school diploma, used to remark upon this degree frequently. I think that's why she married him. He knew why I'd come — he had a grapevine that extended through two valleys — but before I had a chance to launch in, he held up a hand: "Hold your horses. Come here." Obediently I followed him into the untidy, rancid-smelling cabin and down the basement stairs. He turned on the light and showed me a miniature train set-up, the very same trains he wouldn't let Bobby and me play with when we were kids. "Entertainment for young ones," he said, or words to that effect. I missed the point of his remark, too busy staring. There was even a water tower and a station house made with painted ice-cream sticks. A moment later he flicked off the light and led me back to the porch. God in heaven, I swear Ian knew how to throw me off balance. I was unfocused, part of me snagged by a past event that he and I had shared, a time I mostly managed to forget. Back out in the dim light of his porch, I sat on a stump and for lack of any other clue on how to approach my subject, I began to ramble about bank accounts, about money, about the cost of upgrading the End, uncertain as to what it was I *wanted* from him. He sucked a beer and frowned earnestly, nodding occasionally like a man in conversation with himself.

Finally he eased out of the old rocker and, interrupting me, leaned close enough so that I whiffed beer, whisky and something noxious with onions. "You think I was an ass, not making money hand over fist all those years? God dang." He slapped his leg and chortled. The screen door banged behind him.

Now wait a minute, I thought laboriously, like somebody smashed past recovery. Everybody knew that Sam Hill Road's End Resort and Boat Rental was a barely break-even, ramshackle resort that couldn't afford repairs and owed money; everybody in town knew that. This was a mantra I trusted; Christ, I'd grown up with it. In the throes of these thoughts and Ian's comment maliciously reverberating, "making money hand over fist," I saw Jannette out of the corner of my eye. She was like a flash in the outskirts of my consciousness. If her sudden appearance registered at all, it was hallucinatory, because I was burrowing through the years of my using makeshift parts for the boats Ian had me spend my weekends repairing, the hours I'd spent filing and patching and soldering, what Mum called "making do." And then, inevitably, I thought of Mum. All the time that she was going crazy with unhappiness, that cagey bastard was squirrelling money away?

He came out and handed me a jelly glass of whisky. I didn't like whisky, the hard-edged smell of it; I wished I had the courage to toss it in his face. He must have seen Jannette then. "Shit," he said. I looked up from contemplating my glass just as she raised her head and spotted us; and it was as though my startled glance physically reached out and touched her. She wheeled, Jeremy in tow, and beat a retreat. "What was that?" I asked stupidly.

"A mirage. What d'ya think, ya dummy. It was *Ms.* Giffin, what works over at your place, eh. Her."

I didn't know Jannette knew Ian.

"Us old guys have our ways," he said, spitting over the railing into the brown-tipped fiddlehead ferns. "Jesus, lad, it was me suggested she get her tail over to the End. I knew you'd be walking around with your head up your ass and I knew she was the type of woman who could straighten the place around." Here he snickered, wiped his face with the back of his hand like a reprobate in a spaghetti western. He had his act down pat. He practically leered when he said, "I been giving it to her regular, too."

At first I didn't know what he meant — "giving it to her." When I twigged that he was *fucking* her, I was stunned to speechlessness. His dense woods made a run at me. I felt myself flinch. The man could always make me cringe. "Christamighty," Ian exploded, "are you a grown man or what? She's a woman, lad, a lusty woman with a lot on her mind." He snorted. "I see from your face —

always a real secret-keeper, that face, ha ha — that you have a thing for her. Manny, don't bother. She's too old. A low-class broad. Likes it rough. Not your type, laddie."

I was sitting with my hands between my knees, listening to the asshole who had made my mum cry nearly every day. He had sneered at her pathetic efforts to keep herself busy in that godforsaken place. "Why don't you just take it easy and read, Donna?" he'd say and hand her Nietzsche's *Thus Spake Zarathustra*. She'd turned the heavy volume over in her hands, her lips moving, her tongue wrapping itself around the syllables of the title, her cheeks flushed.

He patted me on the shoulder, as if in consolation, and disappeared down the steps. The feeling of being dismissed was familiar, basic and expected. Automatically I stood, shook out my jeans. As a child, I'd depended on him. And even when he had tried to get rid of me, it was about *power*, I realized. I had never understood why he and I made the mad dash to the CP station in Revelstoke, why he wouldn't stop somewhere so I could take a piss — well, shit. I was turning into a teenager, for Christ's sake. *He wanted me by the shorties.* And it had worked.

I started down the trail, lost in thought. About seven months into our bachelor life, he suddenly told me to pack my things and get in the truck. He had an old Dodge Ram 4 x 4. He left Bobby at Occam with some hot dogs and Gatorade and told him to hold the fort overnight. Bobby started crying. Bobby was always crying in those days, he had the slimiest nose in school.

For the whole helter-skelter drive north, Ian didn't say a word. I was twelve, almost thirteen, and scared. When we arrived at the station he bought a one-way child's fare to Toronto while I blinked at my dirty runners in the waiting room that reeked of urine and cigar smoke. We went out to the platform. The wind was blowing and the air had the scent of home, pine and coming rain. By my side was my Boy Scout duffel, stuffed with my worldly goods. I prayed that the Doukhobors had chosen this day to blow up the track for some reason that I was too young to understand. I didn't want to leave Bobby, no matter how he drove me insane with his whining; I didn't want to leave the town of Ruth, or the rough comforts of Road's End, or even Ian himself. As the train — the first one I'd ever seen — screeched and chuffed into the station, he tugged my sleeve. I thought he wanted me to step back to avoid the smoke.

I started towards a crowd assembling near a conductor. I felt the tug again but didn't respond. In my misery, my mind was becoming disengaged, a stance towards life that I was developing. Instead of the gruff goodbye that I expected, Ian tugged at my sleeve again, told me to get in the truck. We marched across the parking lot. "Just don't ever pull that again, laddie," he said, the very words, the truck door closing with a reassuring finality. He turned the ignition and I nodded, didn't have a clue of what it was I'd done in the first place to cause that wild trip or what, in the end, had saved me from falling off the edge of my known world.

I reached the highway out of breath. I was disgusted with myself, the cowardice I carried inside. I wanted Ian banished, I wanted my entire past gone. Nothing about my life had ever been *mine*. I hadn't chosen him, or my mother, for that matter; my whole existence had been foisted on me by adults I hardly knew and mostly didn't like. I was so pissed off I wanted to gnaw bark off trees, but in my present state, if I had tried gnawing bark, I would have apologized to the tree; I was that much of a wuss. I felt the first splatter of rain. Perfect. Now I was being peed upon by the sky.

Driving into town, hair dripping onto my lap, I managed to miss the school bus, driven by Gordie who I knew from rumour was on Prozac. Guys like that shouldn't be driving; hell, since his dose was adjusted and he'd stopped tearing up his goddamn house and scaring his wife and kids, he went around beaming as if some angel with tender claws was perched on his shoulder, whispering in his ear. On the other hand, I thought I could use a dose of Prozac myself; it would be the only way I could deal with what was going on between Jannette and Ian. Sex? He was having sex with her? It was impossible to imagine. Christ, her and buzzardy Ian McDougall?

I parked behind Rundle's Meat and Deli and climbed the stairs to where Deirdre ran her accounting and book-keeping business. The place had the masked pungency of pickled eggs and smoked ham — Dee had air fresheners on the counter and in the washroom, but it didn't help that much, just mixed the deli odours in with Spring-time or Lilac.

"Hi, cowboy," she said when she saw me. "You look like a fella who's been sleeping on a crumpled bedroll far, far too long." She had this way of speaking to me, full of innuendo. Not the words so much but how she said them, one groomed eyebrow slightly raised.

"Yep," I said, going along although my heart wasn't in it, "I am one damp, hongry cowpoke." I emphasized the "hongry." And I winked. It was the way we communicated.

"Well, now, I'll just see what I can do about that, sir. We are at your disposal, we aim to please." She gave me the tip of her tongue and turned around to talk to one of the women who worked for her. I could see Dee shrugging in my direction, probably explaining, and fooling no one, that I was some duty she had to run out for. It was a positive quality she had, a nice way of dealing with people so they never felt she was dumping on them even when she was.

We drove in her Hyundai over to her place, not far, and then dawdled out in the yard, the sexual tension between us building as she walked me to each of her apple trees, touched the miniature apples on them; it was an on year for apples. When she finished tormenting us, she unlocked the back door, turned and stuck her tongue halfway down my throat. From then on, we were moving fast, stripping on our way up the stairs to her bedroom; we hit the bed running. It was so good with her, so natural, it was like the best homemade pasta I'd ever made, it was a wallow in a fine, simmered, totally delicious sauce; we knew each other well, we knew how to please each other. I liked her room, the old-fashioned window shades with round pulls that cast a quaint, burnished light onto the bed; I liked the feel of the nubbly cotton chenille spread on my butt and the wilting coral-coloured sheets, tangled from our lovemaking. I felt a chill, a shiver run through me, and pulled the spread over us, held her close. Her short, stylish hair exuded the aroma of almonds. We were taking a breather before the second round. I ran my hand over her pretty forehead and mentioned Jannette. I thought I was just passing time, clueing Dee in on what had been happening at the End; she knew Jannette was working for me, she'd thought it was a good idea. But I didn't mention the improvements, I started in about Ian and Jannette. It was eating at me, the two of them. My instincts were telling me to be quiet, and I should have paid attention: Joshua Harvey was right; harmony, indeed, was lost, but I didn't know it right away. I mused aloud how bizarre it was that Jannette knew Ian, how bizarre that she'd shown up at his place and then run off.

Dee placed one long leg over my hip and kissed my neck. "Oh, you silly" — and I knew she was going to say something that my basic anal retentive personality did not want to know — "he's poking her. Yeah, that's the way I heard it, honest to God. Mac explained it to me in the bar the other night. 'Yuh, the old fart's poking 'er,' he says. Fun-ny — hey, what's the matter?"

I unwound myself from her, lay on my back, stricken.

"Honest to God, what is it with you? Oh, shit." She sat up on her elbow and narrowed her eyes. "Oh, shit," she said again and gave me a shove. "Give me a fucking break, eh?" She rolled across the bed and sat on the edge, pulling the sheet to cover herself. "You are really bugged by this, aren't you? I've been wondering. Shit. I had a feeling something was going on."

She rose and reached over to the rattan chair, pulled on her tulip-patterned dressing gown and began tying the sash into a perfect bow, the kind you'd use to wrap a special package, observing her fingers working so she wouldn't have to look at me. I watched her, both of us concentrating on her hands. Downstairs the kitchen clock marked the half-hour. When she finished with the sash, she fluffed her hair and sat at her dresser. I might as well have been on a raft at sea, I was so ignored.

She looked at herself in the mirror and had a conversation. "You haven't been over for a while. I tell myself, he's busy being responsible for a change, getting the resort together. Then I tell myself, No, it's something else. Cowboy has got his head in some dilemma. There's a wind blowing through his little noggin. But it's more than that, isn't it? It's that woman with the fat kid. Honest to God. She's a total loser. I thought you'd have more sense. Do you realize what she is?"

"A hard worker." I found my jaw tensing.

"Oh, man." She flung herself out of the chair and stepped back to the bed, slapped the edge with an open hand. "Get out of my house." There were tears in her eyes, but the emotion causing them didn't stop her from scooting over to the bedroom door. "Get out of here, Matthew Fauler. Oh, God. Look at your face. You are in love, cowboy, and it ain't with me." I had tumbled out of bed, was pulling on my jeans, buttoning my shirt. Her woman's mind had leapt way past me. Love? *Love*? I couldn't grasp who she was talking about, but I couldn't get a word in edgewise to get her to stop, either. "How could you?" she was going on. "How could you just come in here like this? Man, oh, man. Get out. Get out of my fucking house." Then I was hurtling downwards. I thought I might puke, but I knew Dee's temper; if I was going to, it would damn well be outside.

I stood across the street from her place for the longest time, sniffing food in the air, remembering things, remembering my relationship with Dee. She had a white picket fence around her little house and clematis climbing the porch. I had helped her sew cushion covers for the living-room davenport. I'd gotten the guys together to haul out the old fridge. I'd cooked great meals in her kitchen. We had thought, at one time, that we were making a future nest. I stood there and waited for her to come out but she didn't; she'd probably call her office, say she wouldn't be in after all. I didn't know why I just didn't take the situation in hand, leap over that picket fence and bang on her door. I didn't. I thought, instead, about how when I was a young lad in high school with a chip on his shoulder, an ache in his heart and a second-hand motorcycle, I decided to sneak out of town, head to Vancouver for a shot at big-time money and hot women waiting to be seduced by a lanky, pensive dude — I pictured myself as both pensive and dudelike in those days. The day I was leaving Ruth for good, I paid a visit to some old folks who lived next door to us before Mum married Ian and before he moved us out to the End. I wanted to say goodbye, I guess, because they'd always been kind. When Mum went moody, they were there for two boys who were wandering the streets. They would invite us in for tea, a tea that was an orange drink, Tang, most likely, but served in proper cups with lemon cookies on plates. It made us feel protected by civilization. Leaving town, I stopped by, and leaning back comfortably on a frayed blue duck-cloth cushion, the rest of me spread out on their veranda, shooting the breeze with the old couple, now dead, about a cornfield, how high it was, how high it ought to be for the time of year, her in a rocker shelling peas and him hunkered on the steps, bony knees wide, wearing the sweat-stained felt hat he always wore, sharpening a fishing knife on a whetstone, I felt happy. That's all there was to the scene, an undercurrent of safety and peace marred somewhat by my upwellings of impatience to hit the road; and the sun was dappling her old hands and the bucket of empty pods, the late-afternoon rays filtering through the grape arbour.

I didn't leave Ruth that day. They invited me for dinner. Meatloaf and mashed potatoes, my favourite at the time. I turned away from Deirdre's and started walking back to town where I'd left the van and I did not fall off the world.

The male contingent of the Fall FunFest committee was meeting in the extension that would eventually be Sam's new lounge. When I joined them, they were chomping through baskets of fries and shooting the bull about the name Sam intended for the lounge. I thought "Lizards" pretty witty, myself, but some of the fellows didn't get it, had never heard of lounge lizards. Freddy from the feed supply said the idea sucked. We drank to that, sniggering. You get seven guys in an unfinished room, sawdust and crud on the floor, windows covered in black plastic — no clean-cut lake-and-mountain scenery reminding you of your spiritual life — and what the church ladies call un-refined behaviour is bound to follow, thank Christ. I drank myself nearly shit-faced. The drink gave me the courage to act on a notion that had started squirrelling around in my brain.

Heading over to Billy Viola's old place by the creek, taking Jannette by surprise, definitely seemed a fine con-cept as I was leaving the lights of the Zoo and the fellows were revving their vehicles for home, calling to each other, honking. The End would be dark and cold and I would have to eat cold cereal for supper because I couldn't man-age fixing anything else and that just seemed a damn shame. I figured Jannette and I would sit by the creek and shoot the breeze. That's all I told myself I was doing, just being a friend dropping by.

Jeremy was sitting outside on the trailer steps when I walked up humming. He drew back when he saw me, as if I were a ghost. "Howdy," I said, probably too loud, but my voice fitted into the part of town where they lived, narrow lots, TVs on full blast, doors open to the warm night.

"You can't go in," Jeremy said, scrambling to his feet. "You have to go back."

Man, I thought, this kid could really be annoying. Little Sir Lancelot. The intuition I was supposed to be developing in myself was once again totally missing; I felt pissed off by this pipsqueak blocking me. That twerp could make my hackles rise simply because he was on the same planet. I didn't notice anything about him, didn't notice that his eyes were red, didn't notice that the porch light wasn't on, didn't notice him hugging himself when I'd first sashayed up. Instead, I squinted at him belligerently. He put out his hands, soft little pudgy hands, as though he could stop me. "She's not feeling well," he stammered. "She's — she's upset."

I didn't even knock.

There are times you should listen to kids, even ones you don't like; and when you're drunk, you should stay home. The screen wheezed shut behind me and instantly I found myself in another world. Chaos. I had walked into a household in shambles. A quick glance showed me an overturned end table, broken, scattered dishes, a lamp knocked onto the floor, bulb still on, shade cockeyed. That was for starters. From another room I heard strange, throaty sounds that I couldn't place. Strangled cooing, moaning sounds. I moved towards them, adrenalin pumped. All kinds of possibilities collided in my head. I thought they'd been robbed, an intruder hurting Jannette.

I forgot about Jeremy outside, I forgot about his warning. I just suddenly knew that some monster was brutalizing Jannette. I sprinted down the hall, threw open the bedroom door. She was there, all right, but the room was so bare, a bed, a pole lamp, a table, that it was easy to see she was alone. She moved her head and saw me but the sounds didn't stop. I saw she held a knife in her hand, what looked like a fish-gutting knife, small and sharp. She was sitting on the foot of the bed, on a stained and saggy mattress, wearing a pink housecoat. The bed sheets were in a heap on the floor. She didn't pay any attention to me as she drew the blade lightly, almost reverently, across the inside of her upper arm, intent on the blood beading along the cut. She didn't wince. There is a certain cold beauty in self-destruction, I knew from personal experience. I didn't dart over and pull the knife from her hand, I stared, transfixed. Now I understood where her keloid scars came from, the ones that I'd noticed on her arms that first day; I understood about her being so-called "accident-prone." It made me sick to my stomach. I must have uttered a sound, because she turned to me a second time. The eyes that looked at me were not those of the Jannette I knew. Or, rather, the Jannette I had invented for myself. This woman didn't seem to recognize me. In a girlish voice she said, "I'm being bad. I know. I can't help it. I was very bad." Then she picked up a bottle of booze I hadn't noticed on the floor and drank from it, held it out to me. "Your old man's been doing me. *Fucking* me. Yeah. You can too, if you want. It's all right. It's you I really like." She giggled. "You're sweet."

As though remembering what she'd been doing, her attention shifted and she began piercing her arm in methodical, delicate jabs.

"Give me the knife," I said. She kept up her meticulous cutting. "Give me the knife," I said louder, and was disregarded again. I was invisible and helpless as her blood dripped down her arm. I felt my sense of myself crumble. My being in the room condoned her sick actions because I was doing nothing, and she was ignoring me; I was a zombie and I couldn't stand it one second more. I just blew. I kicked the door shut, an image of Jeremy alone outside flashing through my mind, and bolted towards her, yanked the knife out of her hand. It slipped and thudded on the floor. She was drugged or stoned or drunk or all of it and didn't seem to give a damn; she didn't react.

"You bitch," I said. "I hate your guts." And I did; instantly my emotions came flooding back and I hated her with such fury that I shoved her, climbed onto her. I moved my hips viciously against her. "You like this, don't you, you like it rough, don't you," and I was struggling to open her housecoat, kneading my fingers down her plush belly, feeling the excitement in myself as I moved towards raping her and her just waiting for it, except I was too smashed to pull it off, my zipper got caught in my shirt. I grabbed a hank of her hair instead and pulled it and pulled it until she stopped being so puking passive, until she let out a shriek and flailed at me and I felt her fists. I let go, strands of her hair stuck to my palms, and fell off her.

I lay on my back, so dizzy I was close to passing out. "You are absolutely unhinged," I said. Beside me I heard her gasping. I looked with interest at my hands, smeared with her blood. She could pick up the knife that was on the floor and kill me if she wanted, I wouldn't stop her. It wasn't half bad lying there, I was aware of floating in a tremendous calm. I found myself studying the patterns in her watermarked ceiling, thinking that trailers always have watermarks, I didn't know what it was with them.

In the next few days, dark thoughts having to do with abandonment, betrayal and control — the original ABCs — wound through my brain like wads of entrails. I holed up in Occam's Cabin with the blinds pulled and thought about my failures the way I might poke through garbage trying to find the bagged celery heart I threw out in a frenzy of fridge cleaning: gingerly, with disgust, and then, after a bit, hands already a mess, I would dig in. I was unwanted — even by my self, if I had one, that is, a real Self, the one with a capital *S*. I lacked control over every aspect of my life, but I still had the power to betray my own best interests, which I was aware of doing with a vengeance. I wasn't answering the phone. People enquiring about accommodations or rates got no response from me. The phone rang surprisingly frequently — a sunny fall was predicted — and the machine clicked on. And off. And rewound. I sat and listened to their voices, how some of them didn't understand about waiting for the beep. Answering machines still weren't all that common in Ruth or the smaller towns around. Old-time Ruthites still tended to hang up quick, even if in the past I had explained the system in great detail, standing in front of the post office or in line at the grocery; or else they said, "Hello? Hello?" expecting an answer. I took pleasure in people's discomfort with my answering machine because I hated the damn things myself. It took courage leaving your voice in limbo, possibly for some stranger to find and judge and conjecture about, just as I was doing sitting in the dark, listening.

The phone rang and the TV showed reruns and occasionally I stirred to pull back the shade and peek out the side window at the tool graveyard and ponder history. I could see the *L* where Occam's Cabin's kitchen had been extended, and the cabin's foundation, constructed of rocks worn smooth by ancient oceans, joined like cells by concrete. A few feet from the crook of the *L* was the start of the partly buried pile that included old tools and rusting tin cans, lawnmower parts, odds and ends of boat motors, vises, general crap. Most was of no use, like a spade from the turn of the century or the hoe with the chipped blade. Alongside the hoe lay a trowel, its wooden handle splintered; a ridging hoe; a three-pronged cultivator, sans handle, that looked like a skeletal hand clutching the soil. There was a rusted sickle attached loosely to its handle, making it, I thought, lethal, obviously from the tetanus point of view, but who knew where the blade would fly off, in what direction, were anyone to take the tool seriously.

On the fourth day, Jannette pounded on the door and shouted, "Get out here, you asshole! There's people here.

I already booked two into Otter for the week. Their cheque's under the front door."

"Go away," I replied. I turned and slunk into the bedroom, where the drapes were closed and the room was musty and dim and had the pong of semen and sheets that badly needed washing. I had been hearing Jannette around the last couple of days, had noticed her car come and go. I sat in the rocker and stared at my scuffed slippers. I got bored with that, wandered back to the living room, stood scowling at the external evidence of my life. Everything was brown: the curtains, the furniture, the walls, the beer bottles strewn about. One corner of the cheque that Jannette had left was visible under the door. I tiptoed over and picked it up. From the amount, it appeared that Jannette had raised the rates. The words "Road's End Resort and Bt. Rntl." managed to get through to me: this place really was mine. The beer and rye bottles and crap food packages — chip bags and smeared bean-dip cartons — reminded me of how like Ian I was. Something in me wanted to take hold and tidy up, but there was that other that refused.

Meanwhile, Jannette was banging on the door again and calling me names. "Wimp! Crybaby! Come on out of there, you wuss!" This woman was impossible to comprehend — chopping away at herself one day and doing business the next. How could anyone understand a person like that? I showered and dressed in fresh clothes. I eased open the heavy front door cautiously, a bear coming out of hibernation. I poked my head out, stepped over the threshold.

Jannette was sitting on the railing at the end of the porch. From all appearances, she'd been there for hours. She contemplated me. I returned her gaze and thought of questions I wanted to ask and things I needed to say to her. Just then a man came around the side of the cabin. He stood on the grass below the porch, took off his cap. "You open? You got a cabin available? Two of us, me and the wife." He looked harried, in need of a vacation. Jannette and I turned to each other. She nodded. I cleared my throat. "You bet," I croaked.

In the following two weeks, as Ruth revved up for FunFest — Road's End Resort and Boat Rental had been talked into sponsoring the annual old-fashioned kiddy soapbox derby — Jannette and I did a lot of work around the place and not much talking. We made flyers to post and Jeremy coloured them. She also started a soapbox for him. He said he didn't intend to ride in it and make a public fool of himself and I could understand why; he was surrounded by adults constantly making fools of themselves. But sometimes he pitched in, handed her slats or screws. Jannette was smoking more. She'd heard from Winnipeg about the date of her custody hearing. And by then I knew she had an illness. A mental illness. She was what psychiatrists informally called a "cutter," a self-mutilator, behaviour that was triggered by self-loathing, self-doubt, lack of self-esteem, the usual. I wanted to know more about why she'd taken that route, how it started; I wanted to know what had transpired between Ian and her and if it was still going on. But to ask her outright would force her to lie; not force her, exactly — I sensed she could lie without giving it a thought, and I didn't need to know that about her nature or to have the lie itself between us.

Friday evening before the big weekend, we were outside Occam, surveying the tool graveyard. My brother, Bobby, and his crew were heading up from Arizona; it would be a madhouse around here soon enough. Jannette looked exhausted and worried and I felt sorry and powerless, both; I hadn't yet figured out what I could do to make a difference in the long run. I lowered my head, screwed up my courage and asked if she would like to go to the Pancake Breakfast with me in the morning. "The three of us," I said. "Separate vehicles." She snorted, didn't reply. I was used to that from her. I turned my attention back to the mess. I was thinking that Ian had run the place as an adventure playground for beered-up, male Albertans; and if they got stuck on the lake — and Judith is a big mother of a lake — because the rope snapped on a Merc outboard, well, somebody'd rescue them eventually and the story would go into the oral history of Road's End, to be embellished and retold by the same gang the following year, only the whitecaps would be whiter, the swells deeper, the clouds darker and the stranded men braver. It wasn't bad for business. What Ian sold was the uncertainty, the shadow of danger lurking in the wilds. I personally thought the contamination from contact with the mildew lining the shower stalls in the dust-ball heavens he'd called cabins was perilous enough, but Ian always said I had a sissy streak. Thinking this, I shook my head and said to Jannette, "I can see picking up some of the junk, but not all of it. The sharp things maybe."

"Whatever." She squinted up at me and added, "We'll meet you at the Legion. Sevenish, eh?"

I nodded, pleased, regarded Jeremy down at the dock, piling stones, an activity that I thought showed some hope for him. I realized that maybe my attitude towards the kid was changing. Which made me think maybe there was something to the theory that our life is what we perceive it to be. Reality, in other words, was our own idea. It would follow, I surmised, glancing around the parts that made the whole of Road's End — the cabins, the outbuildings, the dock, the woods — that it was possible to be crazy as loons and happy as larks at the same time.